The Seeker

A Witness for the Demon Series

By Kevin Wollenweber

"The Seeker," by Kevin Wollenweber. ISBN 978-1-63868-132-8 (softcover); 978-1-63868-133-5 (eBook).

Published 2023 by Virtualbookworm.com Publishing Inc., P.O. Box 9949, College Station, TX 77842, US. ©2023, Kevin Wollenweber. All rights reserved. No part of this publication may be reproduced, stored in a retrieval system, or transmitted in any form or by any means, electronic, mechanical, recording or otherwise, without the prior written permission of Kevin Wollenweber.

This novel is dedicated to
Leslie Rae. She arrived when I was
seeking.

Also
Larry Lard, a true *freak*, but in the
absolute best way!

Preface

Chapter 56: Rage of Ages/ The Keeper-A Witness for the Demon Series /A Witness for the Demon

Satan rose from his throne and summoned his closest legion of Demons. Among them was Orin, a vile, but resourceful creature. With the use of his very thoughts, he commissioned Orin to seek, and find, the one demon who stood in the way of his triumph as god of the Earth.

THE "SEEKER" BEGINS as the demon Orin takes command of a legion of demons and travels up the portal to find and capture the traitor, Gayland. In the final chapter of "The Keeper", Lucifer displays anger and frustration that his majesty has not only been put to the test by the mortal, Alex Dante, but also, by one of his own angels. His anger is consuming him, and he has grown impatient for retribution.

In Chapter One of "The Seeker", we find the demon, Gayland, learning all about the pleasures of his sanctuary and enjoying the peace and security that has been provided, and to which there is no access by his former master. Meanwhile, Chapter Two will reveal how Alex and Courtney Dante are adjusting to the wonders of being parents to their baby daughter, Annabel. Their encounter with Orin leads the vile demon to discover that he must devise a plan, a sinister plan, to use Annabel Dante for evil and the purpose of tracking and finding the coward demon, Gayland.

"The Seeker" is the continuing story of the battle between Angels, humans, and the forces of evil, all colliding and exposing that Lucifer will stop at nothing to achieve his ultimate goal. "The Seeker" will show that the spiritual battle of those opposing forces is firmly in play but under masterful control of the one, and only, God of the universe.

It is my hope that you find this story a blessing and you will become a seeker of the truth.

Kevin Wollenweber

Chapter 1:
Solitude

THE MID-MORNING SUN WAS MAKING ITS JOURNEY to the noon sky. There wasn't a cloud to be seen for miles. He pushed up and away from the antique rocking chair that was placed perfectly on the porch so he could view the horizon and the magnificence of his sanctuary farm. His physical body did not require the rocker to hold him. He was void of any human weight, but he truly enjoyed the sound the chair made as it moved back and forth in a rocking motion against the foundation of the porch. He always pushed the chair when he stood up so it would rock. He likened it to the squeaking tone the hinges make on a fence gate flapping in the summer breeze, void of any lubrication to silence them. He wasn't sure why he liked that noise; he just did.

Gayland walked to the edge of the porch steps in order to survey the jar that contained the water, tea bags, and eventual liquid delight that would fulfill his existence. "Perfect color, it's almost finished," he rejoiced. Adorning the same tattered denim overalls and dirty cowhide boots that his former human host, Jim Johnson, had worn, the demon found comfort in these mortal clothes. Still, he could not let go of the black leather motorcycle jacket that identified his demon persona. So, he placed it over his upper torso despite it not adhering itself to his present ensemble. That same black jacket had significance. It was an heirloom to his body of work from his past. A former past, but a trophy none the less. It was also the element that identified him before the mysterious human, Alex Dante.

The matching clothes he used to wear when he appeared before one of his defeats, Andrea Best, as she twirled her husband's beads in her fingers to mock him, would no longer be remembered. Things had changed for Gayland and he thought it amazing that he no longer held animosity towards her. He could only assume it was because he had found solace and peace from any future torment, here at his farm. These overalls were not covering his physical demon body out of spite or disdain for Jim Johnson. It was just the opposite. He had found respect for the human host. That same host who exposed to him that there were mortals that could see demons, and thus caused him to question the dynasty of his former master. Plus, this mortal gave him a gift, despite Gayland being the agent that delivered him to pain for an eternity. But this was Gayland's farm now. His sanctuary and solitude.

Turning towards the farmhouse, he moved towards the old wood door with the torn screen which allowed entry therein. The old Frigidaire ice box had begun to whine, as the compressor was on its last leg. Gayland had no understanding of human appliances and didn't know what this strange noise was, emulating from this box which held the jewels of his very peace, ice.

Opening the top of the box he took account of the metal trays into which he had poured the liquid water, placed the metal divider with the lever on top, and inserted them all into the top compartment. In a matter of human time, this water hardened and produced frozen cubes. These cubes were now ready, and he collected and inserted them into the mason jar on his porch next to his rocking chair. Gayland poured the fluid that had once caused Demetri so much angst, into the jar.

Gayland laughed as he wondered what had become of the mighty Demetri. Perhaps he had been shown compassion by Lucifer and simply been relieved of his existence. "Now, wouldn't that be too bad for my dear Demetri," he cackled with the sarcasm of an improv comedian. He raised the mason jar to his demon lips. This time his hand did not shake. The light brown tea was cold and as it slid down his throat, he took great delight in the feeling. He had drunk several glasses of iced tea since Dante had offered him solace in this sanctuary. As he finished the last of what was left in the glass jar, he carefully placed it back on the table beside him. Just at that same moment that the jar touched the table, one of the four legs collapsed causing the table to spill the contents of tea and ice onto the porch and shatter the jar into several pieces.

Jumping to a standing posture, Gayland stared at the contents laying on the porch floor. He tilted his head to the left and then the right in a curious fashion. The ice cubes began to create small streams of liquid water as their melting streams bolted for the cracks in the porch floor. It was then that Gayland became worried. "This vessel is obviously broken. It cannot be used again," he fretted. In a panic he didn't walk to the kitchen but moved supernaturally to the area. He had never needed to open any of the cupboards before. There was never the need, until now. Opening the first cabinet he was distressed to discover only ceramic disks. Gayland had seen humans use these disks to place their nourishment upon, but he had no need of these devices. He had no desire to consume food and Alex had not offered this human experience to him.

Moving to the second cupboard, Gayland thought for a moment he might be feeling the effect of human sweat.

He was glad he had never sweated before as it wasn't pleasurable. Flinging open the second cupboard with both of his demon hands placed on the matching doors with painted knob handles attached to them, he breathed a sigh of relief. There before his eyes were several mason jars aligned in rows on each of two shelves. It occurred to him that he must still be careful with each of the jars he utilized because he wasn't quite sure just how long he would be permitted to enjoy his sanctuary before he was forced to leave and join his fellow kind, imprisoned and helpless.

Still, he was relieved to see the abundance of jars and praised his former host, Jim Johnson, for his foresight. Without iced tea, this would not be a complete sanctuary. The iced tea brought him the same pleasure that the Angels of Gabriel enjoyed. Then, Gayland became terrified for the first time in his demon existence. "Where are the tea bags?" he asked, like a sacrificed character in a horror film.

Chapter 2:
Distance

COURTNEY CAREFULLY SPREAD THE BLANKET out to cover the grassy meadow. She motioned for Alex to bring their beloved child, Annabel, to rest upon the blanket as she set their picnic lunch on the blanket opposite of the area from the baby. Her husband gently laid Annabel down on the blanket on her tummy as the baby was still in slumber mode from the drive over to Hillsborough City Park. "This is an absolutely beautiful day, isn't it, Alex?" Courtney gleamed at the surroundings as her voice reflected God's glory in his design.

"Absolutely beautiful," Alex affirmed her observation.

"You hungry yet? I slaved all morning on this picnic lunch just to please you," Courtney asked as she smirked.

"I'm always hungry, my dear. But it pales in comparison to just gazing upon your face in this beautiful place. How did you get this fried chicken into these nifty plastic containers with the Hanson's Market labels on them?" Alex responded with a straight face in an effort not to reveal his sarcasm.Humor was an important foundation for their marriage and Alex and Courtney knew when to be serious and when to keep it light. They enjoyed the chicken, potato salad and fresh French bread while watching little Annabel delight in the new sensations and smells of an Oregon summer. Two sparrows chirped as if in conversation with each other and the aroma of freshly mowed grass permeated the air around the Dante's. Alex, holding a plastic cup containing his favorite pop, root beer, glanced at Courtney. This was one of those moments that he could sense the conversation was about to turn serious.

She carefully extracted a dandelion from the ground and was pondering the bright yellow hues of its flower as she began to speak. "Alex, I think we need to discuss our future. Not yours or mine, but our future as a family. I mean, Annie won't be an infant for long and our home in Astoria is inexpensive, but it's not suitable for our family long-term."

Alex acknowledged her angst. "I've been thinking about the same thing. I knew we would have to have this conversation sooner or later." Placing the root beer on the grass near the blanket to protect against an accidental spill, Alex rolled on his side to face Courtney who still held the dandelion in her hand.

Courtney looked at her husband with her brownish eyes that could slay a dragon with just a simple glance. "You know how much I love you. Not just because God makes me," she smiled with a sheepish grin. "I respect your anointing from our Lord, and I would never question what he has appointed you for in the future, but…" She paused, "I can't help but believe God has something…more…for you here on earth other than conquering demons at the State Mental Hospital."

He could feel the apprehension in her voice. Her words were spoken out of love and caring but she was fearful she had offended her husband. "I have prayed many times for God to reveal his plan for me. More times than you would believe, Court," Alex responded to soften her concern.

"I have an idea for you to consider. Just an idea, not a demand and I don't even know if it would be God's will,"

Courtney softly told him like a shrewd salesperson with a vacuum at his doorstep.

"Tell me." Alex inquired with all curiosity. Just as Courtney was prepared to reveal the contents of her idea, Annabel awoke and would have none of it prior to receiving her scheduled time at her mother's breast.

Chapter 3:
Orin

Sitting on a park bench near a walking path just uphill from the couple and their baby, Orin, the demon, had taken his physical form. Mortal form disgusted him. He was a spirit angel and to reduce himself to this appearance was demeaning. Still, to take on human form was commanded by his god, Lucifer. He had been instructed by Lucifer that there would come moments in his duties that acquiring a mortal persona would aid him. These truths were evident in his past successes and Orin was a loyal member of the legion.

Unlike his fellow hosts of Hades, he did not choose a human form of earthly magnificence. Instead of selecting a persona that was tall, at least six foot two, and muscular to show physical dominance, he selected a short male with ginger features that included a misshapen rough beard about his rounded face. His physique was solid but not muscle bound. Wearing plaid Bermuda shorts and a grey tee-shirt, Orin was inconspicuous and unintimidating. He would never be suspected of being from the revered legion of Lucifer.

Nothing compared in his disgust for human form more than witnessing the behavioral actions of them. As Orin gazed upon the female of his foe in the feeding ritual of their infant human, he was repulsed. "How weak these humans are. They disgust me in their weakness," He spat on the ground in recognition of his disdain.

He was relieved to see that the event down the hill from his view was completed. The body movements and mannerisms of mortals confused him. Orin expected more of this highly feared and revered agent of Gabriel's God. In expecting more, he was curious why more patrons of this earthly place hadn't come over to where he resided with his female and his offspring. "Perhaps he is not as powerful as my master has indicated. I would expect humans to bow before him, as I do my master," he thought to himself with total sincerity. Orin stood up from the bench on his newly manifested earthly limbs. Looking down at the path he realized his mortal feet were uncovered. "Oh yes, feet coverings for this time period are normal."

Utilizing his demon sight, he surveyed other mortals who were roaming about the park to capture an idea on which footwear to manifest for his feet. He made his choice.

As Orin moved forward down the walking path to encounter the mysterious mortal who was commanded by Gabriel's God, he noticed a small black stripe on each of his mortal shoes. "Swoosh! It looks like a swoosh," he remarked to himself.

Chapter 4: Arrival

Cindy fumbled for the keys to the front door of her Hillsborough, Oregon, home while attempting to not drop the several bags of newly bought groceries. She scurried like a mouse to the kitchen to set down the bags and save the contents from spilling. Having saved the day with her quick response, she began to remove the contents from the bag and put them in their appropriate places in the pantry and refrigerator. She smiled in anticipation of her guest's arrival to see her new home in Hillsborough. Although it was not a large distance to her new town from Astoria, roughly one hour as the crow flies, Cindy was grateful that her friends, Alex and Courtney Dante, and their precious child, Annabel, had accepted their invitation to visit and stay with her and Tyler for the weekend.

Just as she had completed putting away the groceries, her husband, Tyler, entered the same front door that she had hurried through just moments before. She was happy he was home. Since accepting the position as lead Pastor at Redeemer Christian Church in Hillsborough, his time had been stretched to say the least.

Tyler advanced towards Cindy and proceeded to kiss her on the forehead, which was his ritual. "Everything ready for the arrival of our honored guests?" Tyler asked.

Cindy grabbed Tyler's face with both hands and placed her lips on his. After releasing her husband from the moment, Cindy responded, "Yes, I think we're ready. Are you as excited as I am to see them?"

He placed both hands on Cindy's shoulders and looked directly into the beautiful alabaster eyes of his wife and replied, "This is going to be a terrific weekend. We have so much to catch up on with them. I would be disingenuous if I didn't confess that I was curious to learn more about Alex's experiences with the demon world."

Cindy smiled and, in a catty way, spoke to her husband, "So, what am I, chopped liver? You know, I have some experience with demons, too."

Tyler tried to display his remorse in forgetting that his wife had firsthand accounts with the demon world. He grabbed Cindy's hands in his and kissed them. Kneeling to her leg that held the remnant scars that the demon had convinced her was the way to peace, Tyler kissed the scars. Standing back up to face her, he had a small tear running down his cheek. "I will never forget what you went through, love. I am so grateful to God that he strengthened you through that and brought you to me."

She brought an open palm to Tyler's face and, with her tender smile, reassured him that she felt the same way. "I know, babe, but my curiosity is not so much about demons. I want to know more about being a mother. I want Alex to discuss what it's like to be a father. I want us to experience Annabel and start to think about being parents."

"You want to have a baby?" Tyler responded with the surprise of walking into a crowded home and people jumping out to wish a happy birthday.

Cindy's eyes grew wide, exposing more of their alabaster hue, and she replied, "If God wants us to! Maybe it's time to start discussing starting a family. I understand you're just getting started at the Church and maybe this isn't the best time…"

Tyler placed a finger on Cindy's lips to stifle any more conversation. "Maybe we pray about it. It's good timing to have the Dante's here with us."

The hug Tyler received from his response was way better than the accolades he received from his congregation regarding last Sunday's sermon. He released Cindy and ran to the bedroom to change into his leisure attire. As he sat on his bed and tied his tennis shoes with the bold black swoosh emblem, he couldn't help but let his mind return to being curious about Alex and the mission ahead of him. Demons constantly occupied his thoughts and his apprehension.

Chapter 5:
Smell

WITH ANNABEL SATISFIED AND RESTING on her mother's chest and shoulder, Courtney returned to her conversation with Alex. "What I was starting to say before little Annie interrupted was, maybe God has more planned for you while we are here on earth than as a ward attendant."

Alex was taken back by Courtney's statement. It took him by surprise, and it was obvious to her that she had thrown her husband a curve ball. "I'm not sure what to say," Alex stared at her with a confused look like she had just spoken a foreign language.

"I was so afraid to start this conversation with you. I imagined you would take it wrong and hate me for it, and I really don't know how to say it to you," she spoke with a careful tone.

Alex moved closer to where Courtney and Annabel sat on the blanket. "Go ahead, honey. Please tell me what's on your mind. I'll do my best to understand and listen to you. Don't be afraid to always tell me what you're thinking."

Courtney knew she had married a man of God. Everything he said and did was as a man should do to honor his wife. She felt a new degree of comfort in expressing her feelings. "I believe what you do at the hospital is very important. You're there for your patients and you care for them with such honesty and compassion. You also care for us, me and Ann, and I appreciate that so much. I just believe you could do so much more for people if you got your PhD in psychology and took your skills to a higher level."

Alex pondered her statement, and with a reverent tone, answered her. "I've often desired to go back to school and do just what you suggest, but now, I have a family." He stumbled for the words to say, "I have to provide for that family and to go back to school would be financially impossible."

Her look displayed the love she had for this man. While she gently rocked Annabel in her arms to continue the child's slumber, she answered her husband with what she was so apprehensive to say in the first place. Looking at Alex, and with the strength of a thousand Angels, she replied, "I have an offer to be the Head of Nursing at St. Paul's Hospital in Boulder, Colorado." There, she said it. The tension in her voice showed heavily to Alex just how hard this had been for her. Courtney examined his face. Alex's eyelids showed no covering of his now fully exposed brown iris and pupils.

The only answer he could possibly muster was, "What?"

"I wasn't really seeking the position, Alex. They came to me. At first, I really didn't think much about it. I'm not unhappy at OSMH, and we're new parents. It just didn't seem like the right time. Especially with your battles with the demon world. Financially we're doing okay but certainly not well enough to send you back to school."

Alex was sure his face still showed astonishment, the same as Annabel's at every new wonder of the world she encountered. "How does moving to Colorado change any of that for us?" he asked with complete curiosity for her answer.

Leaning in towards her husband's ear she whispered, "The position pays..."

Not being sure that he heard Courtney correctly, Alex had to question again what his wife had just told him. Flabbergasted he replied, "Money isn't everything but that sure is a lot of money!"

"Enough that you can be a kept man and go back to school. Enough to find a good nanny for Annabel. We wouldn't be rich but once you're a licensed Psychologist, we would be blessed by God to be very comfortable. And, have more babies," she answered.

Stroking his chin at her revelation, he had to respond, "Ah, this is what this is really about, having more babies."

Courtney laughed while leaning into and kissing Alex. Every kiss he received from this woman was like a hummingbird receiving the nectar of the morning dew.

"Where would I go back to school? I'm not even sure I could get accepted anywhere. I've been out of school for a while."

Courtney placed her hand on Alex's face and answered her husband's apprehension, "You have friends, Alex. I've already spoken with our Chief of Staff, Jon Huggins."

"Jon, my benefactor?" Alex excitedly exclaimed.

"Yes, that Jon," she smiled assuredly. "I told him about my offer and situation. I explained to him that I would really like to consider the offer but it all hinged on you. I told him the only way we could consider it would be if you could get into a good University with a great PhD program for psychology. He told me he'd hate to lose both of us, but he'd be willing to help you on one condition."

Alex could barely speak but managed to reply to her, "And what was the condition?"

She couldn't help but laugh as she replied to her husband's question, "When you get your PhD, you must consider returning to OSMH as a doctor! So, as of right now, Boulder University's School of Medicine is ready to receive your application. Jon arranged it for you."

The joy they both felt at the possibility of a future that God had laid out for them made them feel overwhelmed. "I'll submit my application on Monday as long as you assure me that being a boss is what you want," Alex said.

"I'm already the boss of you so how hard can it be," Courtney replied with a total deadpan face.

They realized that their time here at the park must come to an end as they were expected at the McIntyre home to spend a much-anticipated weekend with their dear friends, Tyler and Cindy. Now, their visit carried even more meaning due to the news they would soon be moving to Colorado. Alex began to fold the blanket as Courtney placed Annabel into her car seat carrier.

As the couple prepared to depart for their car to make the short journey to Tyler and Cindy's new home, a short, red-haired man crossed their path and stopped to chat.

"Beautiful baby. How proud you must be," the man offered up in a way that made Alex uncomfortable.

"Yes, very proud, but we must be leaving," Alex replied somewhat rudely.

The man bent forward as he placed his stubby hands on his knees and smiled an odd smile as he looked at Annabel. It was the type of smile that projected a forced expression, like enemies who meet but are forced into a position of being cordial to each other.

The stranger replied "Too bad you must leave. I enjoy meeting new people here at the park and getting to know more about them."

Courtney looked over at Alex who displayed a concerned face. "Yes, too bad, but we must go."

Alex picked up the carrier that held Annabel and placed his other hand on Courtney's arm to hurry her along. He placed everything into the car in a frantic manner and, after opening the passenger door for his wife, he scurried to the other side, got in, placed the key in the ignition and excitedly put the car in reverse. He glanced at the area where the stranger had confronted them and, despite it being a beautiful sunny day in Hillsborough, Oregon, an unexpected mist had formed to eclipse the image of the man.

As he drove away, Courtney couldn't help but inquire, "Why in so much of a hurry? That man was nice. He was just being friendly."

Alex took one more glance back towards the red-haired man that was no longer visible and answered Courtney, "That probably was not a man. He had a strong smell of sulfur!"

Chapter 6:
A Visitor

AFTER RETURNING TO THE PORCH, Gayland sat in his rocking chair and struggled to consider what he would do if his supply of tea bags were depleted. He had no way to return to Alex, and in a way, was held prisoner on his farm. He was frustrated with himself that he had not spent more time learning about human pleasures, like consumption of liquid refreshment, instead of doing as he was commanded by his former master.

He was startled when a feline cautiously climbed the stairs that led to the porch where Gayland sat. The cat carefully studied his surroundings and the demon who resided in the rocking chair. Unfamiliar with this earthly species, Gayland was curious about what purpose they served. Mortal creatures like these had no reference for him. They did not exist where he came from and thus had no value to Lucifer. All he did know was Egyptians highly regarded them and worshipped their images. He was always curious as to why. These creatures were not Divine.

Glancing up at his porch companion sitting and gazing back at him, the cat plopped down on the porch near Gayland and began grooming himself. Wondering if this feline could see his physical manifestation just like he had learned so many mortals could, he spoke directly to the cat, "I'm not sure if you have sight of me, creature. If you do, I am uncertain why you remain. I was a powerful demon. I am called Gayland. It is a wonder to me that, if you can see me, why are you not fearful?"

Looking up at Gayland, the cat simply replied, "meow," and continued to groom himself.

"Well, I do not observe a soul within you, so I guess you show no reverence, so, there is no way for me to be able to steal it," he answered with a bit of sarcasm. Just then, Gayland was distracted by what he believed was a flash of light emitting from around the cover of the root cellar that was attached to the farmhouse.

He supernaturally traveled to the root cellar and placed his demon thumbs into the sides of the denim straps that held up his mortal coveralls and waited for the event to be repeated. After several earthly minutes, nothing. Cocking his head from the left to the right, Gayland cautiously bent over to lift the cover from the root cellar. The stress on his face was from fear. He understood that the root cellar held the abyssal to another world. A world he was promised could not find him. A promise made by Alex Dante.

"I have been deceived. My sanctuary is not truly mine. My former master has found me and is coming to punish me for my rebellion," Gayland muttered under his breath with a tone of having been betrayed. Slowly lifting the right and left panels to the confines of the root cellar, or possibly the portal to his future pain, Gayland, acting like a frightened child, breached the stairs that led to the room that Farmer Johnson had created to preserve his earthly nourishment requirements.

As he reached the bottom of the steps his mortal boots struck earth and he felt relief. Had this been the portal to his former home he would have felt heat and despair. He could understand as this cellar now permeated a coldness, and no immediate threat. Looking around the room that had been dug into the earth by Johnson, he noticed several decaying wood shelves lining the dirt walls. He was in no need of artificial light to illuminate the cellar. Demons could see just fine in the darkest of places. There on the shelf to his left he noticed several jars, tightly sealed, with mortal fruits and vegetables, suspended in liquid.

Gayland picked up one of the jars to observe it closely. He thought it interesting for a moment and wondered how this human sustenance brought pleasure to the mortals that consumed it. As he went to place the jar back onto the shelf he was startled by a noise and let go of the jar. It crashed to the hard ground and shattered. He looked up at the sun gleaming through the opening to the root cellar to see the origin of the mysterious noise. Standing at the edge of the upper steps was the calico-colored cat who had followed his new farm companion to the root cellar.

Gayland was relieved, but somewhat perturbed, by the appearance of the animal. Breathing a deep, mortal breath, he had received the answer to his earlier question. "I understand you can witness my presence. Unusual for a demon to have a cat, but perhaps you and I can coexist. I have no understanding of you so don't expect me to care for you. I am a demon and only care for myself," he answered like strangers that have been forced together in a trapped environment.

Once he had satisfied his curiosity about the flashing light that brought him to investigate the root cellar, Gayland was convinced it must have been something earthly that illuminated near the cellar doors. As he prepared to exit up the cellar stairs and continue his despair over the dwindling supply of tea bags, Gayland once again was distracted by a flash of bright light. He swiftly turned towards the direction of the light and squinted as a human would at what he saw on one of the root cellars shelves. Moving towards the shelf, he saw that there were several large, sealed jars and it was revealed that they contained an abundance of tea bags. Grabbing one of the jars off the shelf, Gayland tightly clutched it to his demon chest like a running back would hold a football so that he didn't fumble.

Once again, he began his exit up the cellar steps, but this time he strode like a human. He wasn't sure he could travel supernaturally holding his earthly treasure and he was determined not to risk it.

Looking down, Gayland noticed his feline companion was following him back to the farmhouse. The cat glanced up at Gayland and offered his obedience with a subtle, "meow".

Answering back at his new farm mate, Gayland stopped and pointed the index finger of the hand opposite of the one that held the jar of tea bags, "If you think I am going to share my treasure with you, animal, you better think again!" He breached the farmhouse porch and sat in his rocking chair looking out into the eastern Oregon horizon. Gayland now knew the source of the light from his root cellar. The mystery had been solved. Its source wasn't from Hades. It was a promise fulfilled by Alex Dante, the man of Gabriel's God.

Chapter 7:
Plan of Darkness

LUCIFER GAZED AT ORIN in subtle anticipation of the report his servant was about to reveal. He wanted to believe that Orin had already found this obstinate coward named Gayland and was ready to present him. He had spent much of his time planning just how he would punish him. It consumed him just as much as those plans he made for revenge against the mortal, Alex Dante.

Orin did not appear before Lucifer in his human form. In this dwelling place of his master, demons and Lucifer existed on another plain. A supernatural plain. Communication was not commenced in the mortal tongue. Language was available to demons on surface earth, but not here. Lucifer opened the supernatural communication with Orin, "Tell me, commander of my Legion, how have you served me as your master? Please show me the prize you have brought before me."

Humbling himself in a prone posture, Orin responded to his master with a hesitant tone, "I…I have not achieved the goal to which you have commissioned me, lord… yet. I have contacted the mortal to discover how he travels, to track him to the place where he guards the traitor."

Raising his supernatural body from his throne, Lucifer floated around the cavern that was contained inside the only realm where he was lord, Hell. This cavern was devoid of any source of light. It harbored darkness and despair. If there was any natural light it would show rock that was as gray as clay. The cavern had many avenues of entry, but none who dwelled here had desired to come to this abyss. Its occupants were not the social kind. "And did you discover the source of the power that allows him to move as you do?"

Reluctantly Orin replied, "No, I did not. He traveled with his mate and their offspring. They moved…in a mortal manner."

Lucifer had grown tired of excuses and failures from his Legion. He had ordered Orin, his very best, to bring Gayland to him to receive judgement and he had failed. When had his commandments become such a trivial thing to his Legion? First Demetri, then Gayland, and now Orin. He was exhausted at providing second chances for his host. It perturbed him to believe a living mortal could thwart his desires at every turn.

With the heat of his realm causing discomfort to even his spirit being, Lucifer stopped the canvass of his throne room to hover just in front of Orin. "Give me some hope that you can recover my prize should I grant you another chance to please me, dear Orin."

With reverence, Lucifer's commander demon raised his spirit head to address his master, "I would indwell the child of Dante. I would need human time for it to grow in mortal age, but then it would learn of Dante's powers and abilities to move like Gabriel. I would then follow him, as his child, to the place where Gayland exists and betrays you, my lord."

Lucifer pondered the answer he had just received from the demon. Orin lowered his head to the abyssal surface expecting to be vanquished to pain and torment. He also felt the heat of the ground and closed his spirit eyes, waiting for a decision. When Orin opened his eyes, they were no longer spirit. He looked upon his freckled skin, his human skin, that contained follicles of hair with a ginger tint. He was on surface earth, prone on the freshly cut grass of a Hillsborough Park. In the last place he saw Dante, his woman, and his future, drive away.

Chapter 8: Transition

"Colorado?" exclaimed Cindy and Tyler almost simultaneously on hearing the reveal from Alex. Both were wide eyed with the news as Cindy held Annabel in her arms. Courtney had offered her to Cindy to hold as the friends settled in on the McIntyre's new outdoor patio furniture to catch up with each other.

Cindy gently stroked the baby's forehead and Courtney enjoyed watching her friend thoroughly enjoy the moment. It was an amazing transformation to witness, this woman, who once held contempt and anger towards motherhood, now displaying a Godly desire to be one herself. "Well, I must admit, I planned on us having way more that's new to share with you than you guys would for us," Cindy joked as she pointed towards Tyler and herself.

Alex, to diffuse the suddenness of their revelation about moving to Colorado, waved his arms around with open palms to display his amazement with the new home inhabited by his dear friends. "Just look at this place! What a blessing."

Tyler smiled a broad smile and replied, "It sure is. God has blessed us with so much."

Alex, who was wanting to dwell on the recent changes that had been presented to his dear friends, inquired about Tyler's new position as head pastor at Redeemer Christian Church. "How are things going at the Church, Tyler?"

"I believe God is blessing us, Alex. Although it's only been a few months since I took over the congregation, we are seeing some growth. The best thing about that growth, it's coming from new believers."

"I can't think of a better man than you to lead them to the promised land," Alex responded with total sincerity in his answer.

Tyler glanced over at Cindy who was engulfed in loving Annabel and not paying much attention to the conversation. "I appreciate that comment. Maybe the father of my wife would qualify as that better man." Both men laughed at the reply. Cindy sarcastically commented to both jokesters in a response to let them know she was listening to their conversation, "You both got that right, my dad is a way better man than either of you." Courtney couldn't help but acknowledge her friend was correct in her response by nodding her head.

Not wanting to turn the conversation towards a serious content, Tyler crossed one leg over the other and leaned to face Alex directly. "And you, my dear brother for eternity, what is the update on your battle against the powers of darkness?"

Alex quickly looked at Courtney to get acknowledgement that he had her approval to engage in this conversation. He knew that she could become uncomfortable with him sharing his experiences with people who propositioned him. Courtney's facial expressions let him know it was okay to proceed, especially since it was Tyler who was asking. "Honestly, things have been quiet for a few months. With Gayland out of the picture, I haven't had to contend with any of Lucifer's legion at the hospital. It's been almost eerily quiet."

Tyler interrupted to interject and question, "You never told any of us exactly what happened to Gayland. We all know that Demetri followed Satan down the abyssal, but what of Gayland?"

Alex became noticeably uncomfortable at Tyler's question. Having this anxiety was something he shouldn't be feeling considering it was a man of God who was asking. Still, Alex sensed it was best to keep his arrangement with Gayland close to the cuff. "Let's just say that Gayland is no longer a threat to wreak havoc on unsaved souls. He agreed to be bound, and he is."

Tyler was perplexed by the answer provided by his friend but believed it was best to leave further interrogation alone. Cindy, wanting to return the visit to pleasant topics and conversations, returned Annabel to Courtney as she stood up from her chair. "Enough talking about nasty demons, boys. It's time to light the grill and get those wonderful T-bone's a-cookin'."

"Yeah, on a pastor's salary, that's our food allowance for the next month," Tyler explained with a deadpan expression to all. Alex rose from his chair with a large smile on his face to assist Tyler in igniting the grill. He couldn't help but feel that Tyler's comment was meant in jest, but truth be told, he knew it had some merit to it.

Cindy sat next to Courtney as the men went on their way to get the feast started. She had placed a sleeping Annabel in the car seat that also served as rocker and reached out her hands towards Cindy. Placing her hands on top of Cindy's, her friend softly spoke to her, "And you, dear Cindy, how are you?" Courtney couldn't help but notice the scar tissue that was very visible on Cindy's leg. It was a remembrance, to not only Cindy but also everybody who would see the scar, of a more troubled time before receiving God and his grace.

"I feel so blessed, Courtney. Sure, we aren't rich, but God has provided us everything we need and more. Still, I can't help feeling a little jealousy towards you," Cindy answered with a bit of a tremble in her voice.

"Jealousy? Towards me?" Courtney responded with astonishment.

Cindy looked at Courtney eye to eye and said, "Well, maybe jealousy isn't the right word." Struggling for a better word she finally happened upon it. "Maybe envy would be a better word. Yes, that's it, envy. I want to have a baby so bad but I'm not sure Tyler is as enthusiastic. I believe he worries about the evil in this world too much and is afraid to bring a child into it. Or perhaps he is concerned about my past. Maybe he doesn't feel I could be a good mother."

Courtney viewed a small teardrop forming in the corner of Cindy's eye. Her heart sank to hear her friend hurting over the decision to pursue a family with her husband. Hoping to ease the burden that was on Cindy's heart, Courtney held Cindy's hands ever so much tighter and spoke, "I will pray every day that God blesses you and Tyler with a child of your own. As far as any concern about you being a good mother, I don't believe Alex and I would ask you and Tyler to be Annabel's Godparents if we didn't believe you could parent a child."

With her eyes the size of silver dollars, Cindy could barely reply to her friend. "Us? Really? Are you serious?"

Courtney hugged Cindy for what seemed like an eternity, probably because Cindy did not want to let go of the velvet peace that Courtney's arm brought to her soul.

Chapter 9:
Deal

A DEMON NEVER FELT A SENSE OF PEACE. It wasn't offered to them, not deep down. Their sanctuary could provide brief moments in their existence to ponder the magnificence of their benevolent master, but never could they experience true peace. Gayland wondered if peace was what he now felt.

He knew that none of this would last forever. Sitting in his rocking chair, looking out on the deteriorating fields that were once rich with healthy barley, this was pure peace. He knew it. Of course, he had to make a deal with the devil to achieve it, and then he laughed like a horn sounding the end of the work shift, "Wait, I am a devil! How can I make a deal with myself?" he bellowed with delight.

Gayland spent more and more of his mortal time in his physical manifestation. He had come to prefer it over his spiritual being. He had no explanation why since a demon assumed a mortal persona only to interact with humans for the purpose of destroying their souls. Since he no longer had that responsibility, he assumed that it was because he enjoyed the mortal pleasure of a cold liquid beverage, causing him to feel closer to humans than angels.

The earthly sun was making its journey to disappear and usher in the darkness that demons so preferred. A star appeared on the rose and orange horizon and would soon be joined by billions more. The moon would also join them in the sky. He wondered what shape it would be tonight. Sometimes it was round and then sometimes it was different shapes and sizes. He accounted for this as a feat of Gabriel's God. Certainly not his former master's doing.

His gaze upon the confines of his farm were interrupted by the appearance of his calico friend. Bounding up onto the farmhouse porch, the cat had something dangling from his mouth. It strode over to where Gayland was seated and abruptly dropped the contents that were locked inside his teeth. Looking up at his demon companion, he turned his glance towards the prize that laid at Gayland's feet.

A strong acknowledging "meow" suggested that the cat had brought the prize to share with his porch companion. Gayland recognized the dead creature laying at his feet as a rodent. A mouse, perhaps. "Ah, that is correct feline. You are a mortal creature, so you require mortal food. I, on the other hand, do not. You may partake to consume this vile creature all on your own." Hoping it would take its evening meal with it, Gayland motioned for the cat to leave.

With that command from Gayland, the cat grabbed his meal from the floor and carried it by the tail, back down and off of the porch. As he left, Gayland called out, "I admire your hunting spirit. At one time, I was a hunter also. So, I thank you for your token of allegiance." Then Gayland stopped for a moment. He was startled by the response that had crossed his lips. He had spoken the words "thank you." These words were foreign to him. Gratitude was not "demon"!

Just as he struggled to shake off what had just happened, the cat returned to the porch licking his mouth and front paws. It walked over to where Gayland sat once again and, with one continuous motion, jumped onto the lap of his companion demon. Startled and bewildered by this action, Gayland felt the weight of the cat on his lap. It confused him. He had never felt the weight of any creature upon him. There had been the feelings that accompanied indwelling, but this was totally different. Then something occurred that this demon had no explanation for. A noise started to vibrate from the feline that Gayland could feel upon his demon legs. The vibration was exhilarating, and he marveled at the feeling. It was almost as pleasurable as his iced tea.

Not understanding what to do next, Gayland did the only thing that came to his demon mind. He placed his hand upon the feline creature to amplify the sensation he was experiencing. In a natural response, his hand began to stroke the fur of his companion and, as Gayland watched, his companion closed his eyes in apparent contentment of this reciprocation.

Chapter 10:
Communion

TYLER EXTENDED HIS HAND TO ALEX in appreciation of hearing the news about being asked to be Annabel's Godparents. With Cindy's prodding of her husband to affirm the request, Tyler answered with a broad smile, "We would be honored and blessed to be Annie's Godparents. Well, perhaps I should first discuss this with my wife. I am not so sure she shares my delight." A group hug and a prayer by Tyler followed accompanied by tears that fell from everyone in rejoicing and laughter.

The friends sat on the summer patio of the McIntyre's home enjoying the food and companionship of each other. As the summer sun began to yield to the night, Courtney and Cindy moved into the house to place Annabel into the crib for her slumber. Courtney laid the baby on her back, and she and Cindy softly closed the door as they left Annabel to dream. "It was so kind of you and Tyler to purchase a crib for Annie," Courtney whispered to Cindy.

Reaching out to grab Courtney's hands into hers, Cindy responded, "We had hoped to have many more visits from the Dante's and decided to make it as easy for you as possible by having a place for Annie to sleep."

Courtney's face displayed a frown that matched the disappointment in her voice, "Now I feel bad. Leaving for Colorado and all. Can you return it?"

Looking directly into Courtney's eyes, Cindy responded with tenderness and genuine love for her friend, "Don't feel bad. I bought the crib totally out of selfishness. I fully expect to use it for my own child. I kinda figure it'll help move Tyler along in this baby thing!" Both women giggled as they walked down the hallway to rejoin their husbands outside.

"Have you and Cindy discussed having a family?" Alex posed the question towards Tyler.

Tyler turned his gaze towards the sunset before returning it to look at Alex. "Sure, we talk about it often. Cindy's very eager."

"But you're not?" Alex interjected his perception into Tyler's answer.

"It's not that I don't want to have a baby and start a family, I love my wife and would try and give her anything she wanted, it's just…"

Alex waited patiently for his friend to complete his thought. Finally, Tyler was able to bring his answer to fruition, "It's just, I don't know how much more time we have on this earth. I truly believe the evil we are seeing manifested everyday reveals just how close we are. These are the end times."

With a bellow of a laugh, Alex then tried to calm himself down so as not to seem disrespecting of Tyler. After a few moments, Alex was able to speak to his friend with a serious attitude, "Forgive me, Tyler. I meant no harm in my response. Trust me, I have been face-to-face with Lucifer. He is frightened because he knows the events that are unfolding will reveal his fate. Some of those events he has caused, and some, well, he has been caught by surprise."

"Yes, you, above anybody else, would have a sense of the coming times," Tyler responded.

"Not above anybody else, Tyler. Jesus knows but, even though I have had my responsibilities laid out for me, I do not know the day or time. I live my life as every human being should. Doing my best to be blessed by my Lord and Savior. His grace is sufficient for me. If having more children with Courtney is his desire, who am I not to take advantage of that blessing. Even if it ends today or tomorrow."

Tyler smiled back at his friend and posed his question with a seriousness of thought. "Do the demons ever threaten your family?"

"All of Lucifer's minion hate us, but they have no power here on earth with those of us that believe. The young ones who are not at the age to make a choice are protected. I am sure Lucifer doesn't mention that to them, and if a demon were to make that mistake, well, it wouldn't be pleasant," Alex's answer provoked deep review in Pastor McIntyre's eyes.

Courtney and Cindy rejoined the men outside. Both women sought the comfort of one of the arms of their husbands draped over their shoulders as they welcomed the display of a billion stars. The peace and comfort that came with the communion of these brothers and sisters for eternity brought a distraction, for the moment, to all the evil that lurked out there in the darkness.

Chapter 11:
Defile

STANDING OUTSIDE OF THE DANTE'S ASTORIA HOME, Orin remained in his spirit form. He floated back and forth in front of the meager cottage in deep contemplation of just what his next move would be. He was delighted in his resourcefulness at finding their domicile. Still, he was hesitant in his next move. Could he enter this place? Or was it protected with the shield of Gabriel, just like their souls?

His hesitation needed to end. He had nothing to lose. Even if this dwelling had protection and vanquished him, he knew he must still try. Either way, his master Lucifer would punish him if he weren't successful, and that would be equal to the pain he would have to endure in Hades. As he moved towards the front of the house, he advanced with vigor. In the next instance, he found himself standing in what was a small mortal kitchen. He marveled at his success as he scanned the area he now occupied. "How quaint and unbecoming of this mortal who so many of my kind will not speak his name out of fear," Orin muttered in an act of impugnation.

Knowing that Dante and his mate could not be indwelled by his kind and that Dante's kingdom was not off limits to his curiosity, gave Orin a sense of confidence.

The offspring of Dante was not of the intellect to follow Gabriel's God, so certainly it was fair game. Now, within the confines of this mortal's chambers, it would be ripe for the taking and he could remain close to the enigma that was Alex Dante. Biding his time, learning just how this mortal behaves and moves like an Angel. Most importantly, this indwelling would offer him time. Time to save himself from the wrath of his god.

Wanting to know the entire floorplan, Orin propelled himself into the bedroom. He surveyed the apparatus where Dante must retire because he required human sleep. "Human sleep," he croaked in a mocking tone. Orin considered sleep by humans to be a trait that made them less than Angels. Mortals are a creation of Gabriel's God which showed just how flawed and inferior of a God he had become. Orin came to the corner of the room that contained the sleep chamber for the offspring. He ran his spirit fingers over the wood and spindles that formed the sides of the crib. When he indwelled this child, he would be in the same room as Dante and his mate. He would observe their every move. That repulsed him but he understood it was the plan he must follow.

Orin heard a noise outside the domicile of Dante and quickly appeared outside to investigate. Hovering there were several of Orin's legion under his command.

He addressed them with anger, "Checking to see if the mortal's palace was a place of protection and perhaps your leader had been vanquished back down the abyss, have we, my fellow angels? Looking to see if it was your time to step up into my place? So sorry to have disappointed all of you."

One of the demons that had gathered there but was not one of Orin's Command spoke without human words, "No, mighty Orin, I am he that directed you here. I have followed Dante from the mortal hospital where he serves. I have followed him many times before. I wanted to make sure this was the place where Dante and his mate retreated. It is my desire to serve you and our master."

Orin rose above the legion that had gathered before him and laughed with the thunder at a decibel that only demons could hear. Pointing at the demon who had just, moments before, come forward with acknowledgement of allegiance, Orin proclaimed to the multitude of demons, "Lazy! That is what all of you call the servants of my master that go about their soul harvesting at Dante's hospital. Most of the demons that fled that hospital upon knowing of Dante's defeat of the mighty Demetri were frightened. This right here is a demon after our master's heart. A demon after my own heart! One that has proved his mettle and did not flee." Orin motioned for the demon to approach him. "You have served our god and me well, angel. From this time on you shall be my direct servant. These other vermin gathered here shall answer first to me, and then to you!"

There was a great mumbling amongst the legion. None of it sounded as if Orin's command to the multitude had been accepted. "SILENCE!" Orin's supernatural voice penetrated their demon ears like a sonic boom. Turning his attention to the demon next to him, he asked, "What does my master call you, angel?"

"Ignis is my name," the demon answered.

The smile returned to Orin's demon face. "Fire! Our master has named you using the human language of Latin."

"Yes, my lord," Ignis nodded.

"Well then, Fire, soon my prize will come to dwell here, and you will be in command while I am indwelling and defiling Dante's child."

Chapter 12: Venture

ALEX SAT IN A SMALL LEATHER CHAIR in front of the desk occupied by a man he deeply respected, Chief of Staff, Jon Huggins. Pushing a candy bowl forward towards Alex, Jon motioned for Alex to take some candy. "Lemon drops. One of my many weaknesses."

Not wanting to be rude, Alex grabbed a few of the lemon candies in his hand and inserted a piece into his mouth, all the while smiling at Jon. "I really appreciate you taking the time to see me today, Dr. Huggins," Alex spoke with an air of complete appreciation.

"Please, starting today, just call me Jon," he interrupted Alex, as he placed the candy bowl back on top of his desk. Not one to be able to resist a good lemon-drop candy, he plucked a couple from the candy bowl and placed them in his mouth. Alex thought it somewhat funny that they were engaged in a professional meeting and speaking to each other with hard lemon candies rolling around in their mouths.

Alex continued the conversation despite having a mouth full of candy. "Jon, I am so grateful for everything you have done for me here at the hospital. You gave me my job when I graduated from college, you set me up with a place to live, and I will forever be in your debt."

Jon smiled a broad smile as he replied to Alex's tribute, "I appreciate your gratitude. I know there have been moments when your superiors have come to me regarding your religious beliefs. Most of the time they approached me, it was with malice. But I always trusted you, Alex. I'm not a man of faith myself. Still, in all those instances, all I can really decipher is that you're a man of strong beliefs and you stick by them."

"Thank you for that, sir. I mean, Jon," Alex replied.

"So, have you completed your admission packet for Boulder University's PhD program?"

Alex reached inside the leather case that Courtney had purchased for him and handed the papers to Jon. Slipping on his glasses, Jon perused the application and, nodding his head in approval, reached inside his desk drawer and pulled out a letter and handed it to Alex. The contents of the letter were a glowing endorsement to accept Alex Dante to Boulder University's PhD program.

"This is more than I could ever have hoped for, Jon," Alex responded.

"Good, then give my letter of recommendation back to me and I will have my secretary send the entire packet by Federal Express today. After all, you are soon to be unemployed, so, I know saving a dime here and there is necessary," Jon offered in humor.

Handing the letter back, Alex couldn't resist mentioning the upcoming departure of his wife and staff nurse, Courtney Dante.

"Ah yes, Courtney. Not sure she is Head of Nursing material but apparently some hospital in Boulder believes so," Jon offered up with a tongue in cheek mannerism.

Both men delighted in the joking conversation they were having but the affairs of the Mental Hospital required them to return to their professional duties. After leaving

Jon Huggins' office to return to his duties on Ward 11, Alex saw, from the corner of his eye, a short, red-haired man with an attempt at growing a beard standing at the hospital office counter. The counter was behind glass, the type with the wire running through it that created diamond patterns. The red-haired man spotted Alex as he began down the hallway that allowed access to the different hospital wards. Upon catching the eye of Alex, the man smiled eerily and raised his hand as if to say hello.

Alex did not respond to the gesture offered by the man. He immediately recognized him as the same man from Hillsborough Park that had stopped to admire Annabel. He wasn't sure why he revealed himself to Alex here at the hospital. But he knew this was no ordinary man. Demons had come and gone from this hospital. But none had followed him here before.

Chapter 13: 1984

MOTORCYCLES MEANT EVERYTHING TO CHAD. Harley Davidson motorcycles were really the only motorcycle on this planet as far as he was concerned. Having the chance to get out onto the open road consumed him. He loved riding the Harley Softail motorcycle which had just been made available to the public and of which he was now a proud owner. Chad Perryman was a quiet and private man. He preferred the company of only himself and his motorcycle. The motorcycle and road called them to be together, to ride, and he must go.

Chad Perryman was six foot three inches of what many of his female relationships would term "a real man." He was muscular built with long blond hair and beard. He appealed to women simply from his muscular build and handsome good looks, but he, for the most part, attracted women because he projected that bad boy image. Most of the women that circled Chad's sphere of social existence liked "bikers." Chad was the prototype of a "biker dude". The problem that confronted him with every woman whom he started a relationship with was that he was a quiet man. Conversation was difficult for him. Women grew tired of his quiet nature and quickly moved on. Chad desired the company that women brought to a relationship but, he just didn't know how to talk to them. Except for Rita Pinon.

Rita was a firecracker, as many who knew her referred to her, which helped explain her boisterous personality. She was funny, smart and could talk a person's ear off. Rita was the exact opposite of Chad. The term "opposites attract" described Rita and Chad's relationship. She had enough communication for both, and this suited Chad just fine.

The physical part of their relationship never lacked in mutual participation. Rita was always willing, and Chad was happy to oblige. For him, Rita was the perfect woman, and he fell in love with her. Chad had never found a woman that would stay with him, until Rita.

Chad had met Rita at a local motorcycle club gathering in Damascus, Oregon. The club met once a month at a local bar that catered to bikers. It wasn't a particularly fancy bar, but that was perfect for the clientele that patronized it. The one thing this bar did have, that no other bar could offer, was a beautiful setting along the Clackamas River. Bikers would ride their motorcycles along twisting and turning roads along the river. Mature pine trees and moss engulfed boulders postured the slopes of the mountains that lined the road creating a sense of wilderness and adventure.

A dirt lot appeared out of nowhere, positioned in front of an aging log building. Contained upon that dirt lot were various motorcycles of all different makes but most were Harley Davidsons. In the windows at the front of the building were several neon beers signs. In this bastion of rugged beauty along the Clackamas River, adorned with massive forest trees, was a little slice of biker heaven. A place where bikers could meet, drink, shoot pool and discuss the only subject Chad was comfortable discussing with anyone, motorcycles.

The day Chad first laid eyes on Rita she was with a group of people on the patio seating area at the front of the bar. Chad didn't know anybody in the group, but that wasn't unusual, as this bar attracted many new faces. He knew that he had never seen her here at the bar before. As he rolled his motorcycle to a stop in the neatly structured line of other bikes, Chad pushed down his kick stand, slid his left leg over the seat of his bike and stretched as he unzipped his black leather jacket exposing the muscular physique underneath. That's when he first saw her. Rita noticed him immediately. Her eyes tracked him as he pulled into the dirt parking lot until she was certain he was staring back at her. Rita was all of 4"11' in bare feet. She usually wore black leather boots with heels that made her appear taller. Rita's jet-black hair was pulled back into a ponytail. This hairstyle exposed her slender face, with high cheekbones, and enchanting deep brown eyes. Chad was indeed staring at her. She was gorgeous and stood out from the crowd of bikers, and their women, and the forest that surrounded the bar.

Rita turned her head back towards her companions at the outdoor patio table upon detecting that this biker, that had just arrived, was staring at her. It didn't bother her that he was staring at her because she was also interested in him. Rita just didn't want it to seem too obvious.

As Chad entered the bar, he met, and greeted, several of his usual club companions. His group had quartered off a section of the bar and he sat down on a stool amongst them.

"Hey Chad, can I get you a beer?" one of his buddies offered.

Chad answered, "No, but you can get me a sarsaparilla."

Not being known for having a keen wit and sense of humor, it took a moment for the group to respond. When they finally did, it was with roars of laughter. Chad pushed himself up from the bar stool he was sitting on and called out to his friend, "Thanks anyway, I need to pee first. Long ride up here. I'll get myself something when I come back."

The group acknowledged Chad's answer as he walked towards the men's restroom. A short time later, Chad emerged from the restroom and headed towards the bar to order a beer. Standing at the bar was Rita with glass in hand and looking to get a refill. Chad couldn't help but notice her. She had on tight black leather pants with a tank top equally sized to show the contours of her body. Chad moved in behind her and squeezed into the space just to the right of where she was standing. He smiled as their eyes met. The bartender asked Rita, "What can I get ya?"

She glanced back at Chad, whose eyes were still fixated on studying the beautiful woman standing next to him, and replied, "I'll have whatever this man standing here next to me will buy for me."

On that day, neither Chad nor Rita would return to their companions. The day turned to dusk and together they shared their stories of the love of riding motorcycles. This topic of discussion made it easy for Chad and he felt no apprehension about talking with the beautiful woman he had only just met. The following morning Chad woke up in his apartment with Rita, smiling and holding a cup of coffee, wearing only Chad's black leather jacket.

Chapter 14:
Stages

HE WALKED IN THE FRONT DOOR of their Astoria bungalow and placed his keys on the hook that was designated to hold them. Alex looked around the room and was surprised to see several cardboard moving boxes strewn about in various stages of getting filled. Courtney was standing at the kitchen sink washing dishes and turned to smile at her husband. Walking up behind her, Alex placed both hands on her shoulders and kissed her on the cheek that was turned towards him.

"I'm surprised to see this much packing done. I thought you were going to take off a little early to get started with the packing. This looks like you've been at it all day," Alex inquired with a tone so as not to seem too inquisitive.

Courtney turned from doing the dishes to face Alex and explained, "I'm done at the hospital. Jon met with me this morning and assured me that he, and everybody, would miss me desperately, but he knows just how big this move is going to be and he also knows my heart and mind wouldn't be in my work. So, I am done. He also approved paying me for the next two weeks."

"Funny, he didn't mention it at all when I met with him this morning! I guess he forgot I'm your husband. Besides, I'm way more valuable to the hospital than you," Alex snorted in a humorous manner to get her goat.

Courtney tilted her head in a mocking fashion to counter Alex's arrogant comment. She reached out to embrace her husband around his torso and replied, "Well, the truth is that tomorrow is your last day too. Huggins decided to let me tell you myself because he knew you would probably object to leaving today. He anticipated that you would need to say goodbye to your patients. Especially Mr. Sinclair. After all, you are his manservant."

Alex was speechless. His mind was racing with all the thoughts of his time at the hospital and that they were coming to an end. They were bittersweet thoughts. His time as a ward attendant had been filled with many events. Some good, some bad. Some Angel, some demon. "Jon was probably wise in his evaluation. I wouldn't go without saying goodbye to everybody, but Steven Sinclair is going with us, correct?"

Courtney laughed as she gave him a quick peck on the lips and released him from her embrace. "I already turned in your resignation to the Sinclair's. They're disappointed, of course, but the one I'm really worried about is the Queen."

Alex nodded in agreement to her statement and pivoted around the room as though looking for something. "Where is Annabel? Is she asleep?"

Courtney paused in her reply to Alex and then responded to his question with a smirk, "Annabel? Who's Annabel?"

"Oh, I don't know, maybe a small little thing we need to pack to take with us," Alex answered with a smug response.

"I let her stay at daycare. When I forced you to give me the car today and take the bus home, I thought about picking her up, but decided I could get so much more done with packing if I could stay focused," Courtney admitted.

"Good idea," Alex agreed.

Picking up a succulent plant and examining it, wondering how they would transport it and all the various houseplants they owned, Alex said to Courtney, "Well, I'll go pick her up and let you have your last few moments of glee while packing."

"Thanks, honey. That would be great. Or, instead, we do have a few minutes. We could celebrate our freedom from employment," Courtney offered with a wink of her eye.

A short while later Alex wanted to fall asleep, but he understood his daughter needed to be retrieved. As he looked for his jeans, he glanced at Courtney smiling up at him from the bed. He never failed to recognize her beauty. God may have anointed him to be the "keeper" for the demons, but she was his reward. His blessing. Suddenly her smile turned to a frown. Alex, perplexed, asked, "What's the matter, Court?"

Turning in the bed she seemed reluctant to answer his question, but she knew it was best to reveal the burden on her mind. "Your coffee percolator…"

"Yes?" He replied in affirmation, acknowledging that he understood the appliance to which she was referring.

"It died! It won't make coffee anymore," Courtney explained in a solemn and remorseful way.

Chapter 15:
Leather Jacket

GAYLAND REMINISCED AS HE RAN HIS DEMON HAND over the soft leather of the human jacket that was part of his mortal persona. Since accepting Alex's offer to spend the remainder of his earthly days here in the solitude of his farm, void of any threat from Lucifer to bring him torment or worse, Gayland had discovered that his physical responses to stimuli had increased. He felt the drops of condensation fall on his demon hand from the mason jar, felt the cool liquid of the iced tea slide across his demon tongue and down his demon throat, and felt the soft fur as he stroked his feline companion.

The feel of this human jacket, its velvety smooth surface adorned with an occasional crack in the leather due to age and wear, brought Gayland great delight. To be able to experience this sensation was a bonus. One that was not expected by Gayland but was welcomed. The more he lived in this sanctuary and away from the evil that had been his master, the more pleasure was provided to him.

His fingers released the leather jacket and moved towards picking up the mason jar filled with iced tea. As Gayland brought the jar to his lips, he remembered the events that led to this trophy of the black leather jacket becoming his possession. He had coveted this jacket from the very first time he saw it. It belonged to a man who rode the iron machine that mortals called a motorcycle.

Saying that he was a demon that found any human physically interesting to indwell would be untrue. Perhaps it was because of his mission to shadow the mysterious Alex Dante from a young mortal. He wished he could have just indwelled Alex. He found Alex fascinating. That was when the young human man who wore the black leather jacket came to be his to indwell.

Before Gayland's appearance to the young Alex at his father's gravesite, he had yet to manifest his human presence. He couldn't decide what to look like when he did finally expose his physical body to Alex. The biker, Chad Perryman, provided that persona. Gayland did not care to spend any time recalling his triumphs or losses in soul gathering for Lucifer, but Chad resonated with him to use as that example. The leather jacket represented who Gayland would be, from that time on, when he first appeared to Alex Dante, and now, sitting on his porch drinking iced tea from a mason jar.

Chapter 16: Underestimated

HOVERING OUT OF SIGHT, Orin was disturbed to see the activity he was viewing emanating from within the retreat of Alex Dante. It appeared to his demon intellect that this mortal was preparing to abandon his dwelling. Summoning Ignis to his side, Orin questioned his demon companion, "What is this that I am witnessing? Is the mortal preparing to retreat from this place?"

Ignis answered, "Yes, it has become known to me, and my fellow angels that inhabit the place where Dante serves his fellow humans, that he will no longer be present there."

"So, they no longer find him useful? Dante has fallen from grace and is being banished from there?" Orin smugly replied to Ignis.

"On the contrary, my lord, Dante and his mate and child have chosen to leave on their own."

Perplexed by the answer he had just been given, Orin turned his attention from Ignis back to Dante's dwelling. "Perhaps he senses me and is fearful of my power? He has determined that retreating from me would be the best course of action?"

"Yes, perhaps, but, if I can be so bold as to offer this to you my greatness. Dante defeated Demetri due to Demetri's underestimating the mortal's abilities."

Orin emitted scorn that was akin to a fire just having gasoline poured upon it. "DEMETRI was a fool and deserved to exist in torment for eternity! I am not Demetri! I am the Commander of our god's legion for a reason!"

Ignis humbly bowed before his Commander and replied, "Forgive me, lord. I have spoken out of ignorance."

Orin relaxed from this statement by Ignis. "I understand your concern for me. I also recognize that is why our master named you 'Fire'."

"I am here to serve you and our master, my lord." Ignis responded in a tone of allegiance.

Orin pondered which direction he should now go. With Dante leaving this place, should he accelerate his plan to indwell the child soon, prior to the departure of the mortal to his new sanctuary, or perhaps, follow them there? His concern was magnified by not knowing if Dante's new dwelling place might have protection that this place does not. Either way, he must decide quickly.

Orin noticed Alex arriving back at the dwelling. Not wanting to alert Dante to his presence, he retreated far enough away to not provoke suspicion. Just before departing, Orin glimpsed the prize of his plan being extracted from the car. He thought to himself, "How weak this mortal must be. He does not have the power to move like myself. He must utilize this human contraption to travel." It was then that Ignis' words entered his demon mind, 'Dante defeated Demetri due to Demetri's underestimating the mortal's abilities'.

Shrugging these words off as paranoia, Orin could see the face of a young female child being carried to the door by Dante. He was disturbed to see an unearthly glow surrounding the child. For a short moment Orin thought he witnessed the Archangel Michael walking with Dante. Though he did not fear Dante's power, he greatly feared Michael's.

Chapter 17:
Barriers

Rita Pinon had many male relationships before she hooked up with Chad Perryman. She understood she was always attracted to the muscular, quiet type and Chad was no different. She also realized that as much as she preferred to be the communication leader in the relationship, that role also grew old after a time. Rita didn't mind being the partner that initiated an intellectual conversation if the other party engaged at least a little. Unfortunately, Chad wasn't that partner.

She had recently lost her job working at a small convenience store. She didn't mind the work. It involved customer service for the most part. That involved checking customers out as they paid for their merchandise and that allowed her to talk with patrons consistently. Rita felt being able to engage with customers while she was at work sufficed for the lack of communication stimulus when she was home with Chad.

The owner of the store lost his lease when a new landlord decided to go a different direction with the property other than a convenience store. The store owner decided he had enough, would retire, and with that decision, Rita's job went away.

It was autumn of 1985 in Oregon and jobs were not plentiful. As perky and friendly as Rita's personality was, she just couldn't find any work. Nobody was hiring. Rita was fortunate to have Chad to depend upon as he not only paid all the bills, he also provided a place for them to live. The one-bedroom apartment that sat atop the garage of a friend of Chad's wasn't, by any means, luxurious. The apartment was in the town of Damascus which was a small rural town located on the route a person would drive heading towards Mt. Hood. Damascus wasn't located conveniently to any major town or city so that helped to compound the lack of employment opportunities.

Rita did the best she knew how to make it a home. Comfortable surroundings were not a forte Chad possessed. If he had his druthers, he wouldn't own any kitchen utensils so he wouldn't have to wash them. With Rita taking up residence, things became much more domesticated.

Chad worshipped Rita and gave her comfort when she lost her job, assuring her that he would take care of everything. That commitment from Chad did bring her comfort, for a while. He worked at Jensen's Automotive in Estacada as a mechanic and a welder. Jensen's wasn't a large garage, but they had a great reputation for being fair and fixing the problem when a customer had automotive issues. There wasn't anything Chad couldn't fix, and the owner knew he had one of the best mechanics in Oregon with Chad. The owner didn't always pay him like he was the best, but Chad was loyal and liked routine.

With the success of the garage, partly due to Chad, they were quite busy. It wasn't unusual for a customer to have to wait two weeks to even have their car looked at. If Chad was sent on a welding assignment, which was great money for the owner of Jensen's, the wait could be even longer. With the backlog created by their success, Chad had all the overtime he could manage. Overtime was great in Chad's opinion since Rita was not working. It helped to pay his bills, and hers also. The only bad thing was the overtime kept Chad away from home and providing any companionship for Rita.

As time went by, the loneliness that Rita felt began to compound more and more. When Chad did get a day off, which was rare, all he wanted to do was sleep. Sometimes he would offer to take Rita on a ride through the winding forest hills of Estacada, but she knew Chad missed riding his bike more than just spending time with her. When she did try and push Chad into talking about her life and how lonely she was, he would usually fall asleep. Rita was becoming more alienated and disillusioned about her relationship with Chad and it wasn't showing signs of improvement.

It was on a run of working ten straight days of twelve hours per day that Chad entered the apartment to find Rita deep in sorrow. He placed his lunch pail on the kitchen table and laid his black motorcycle jacket on the back of a chair next to it. Chad did not take delight in her red swollen eyes caused by an extended time of crying. Although there was no delight in seeing Rita so sad, Chad knew why she had been crying.

"I know, Rita. I know how hard it is for you to spend all your waking time alone. I just don't know what I can do about it," Chad tried to display as much sympathy as he could show. Rita's depressed state turned from deep despair to lashing out in anger. "You have no idea how it is to spend every day in solitude! You get to leave every morning! You get to spend every day with other people! Even when you get to come home and spend time with me, you're either too tired to talk to me, or you just have nothing to say!"

Chad couldn't argue with her on this statement. Even when things were better between them, he was not a deep conversationalist willing to share wants and needs or emotions. Tonight was no different. Even if taking up sides against Rita and starting an argument would be at least a means to engaging in conversation, albeit not a positive one, the truth is, Chad was just too exhausted. He turned from Rita in her moment of anger and despair and made his way to the bedroom. Stripping his dirty work clothes off and dropping them to the floor, Chad could not even summon the energy to take a shower and collapsed on the bed and fell immediately to sleep.

The last thing Chad heard was the continued sobs of a broken woman. He knew how to fix anything with a motor, but this was something he had no idea how to fix. The only thing Chad could hope for was that tomorrow would be better. He decided he would do something he usually never did and that was to call out sick from work tomorrow. He would rest tonight and spend tomorrow with the woman he did truly love.

In the wee hours of the morning Chad rolled over in their bed. He was careful not to turn to quickly and have the movement awaken Rita. As he settled into position Chad reached out to gently touch Rita's back, knowing she would most likely be turned away from him in their bed. Feeling emptiness, he lifted his head up ever so slightly to confirm his suspicion. Rita was not in bed.

Chad gingerly rolled from their bed and in the darkness of the night stumbled over his clothes that he had hastily dropped on the floor several hours earlier. He moved to the bedroom doorway and out into their meager living room expecting Rita had angrily decided to take up the couch as her bed for the night. As Chad reached the room his eyes became adjusted to the darkness just enough to see that Rita did not occupy the couch. Walking over to the only lamp this small apartment required to illuminate it, Chad turned on the lamp. Glancing around the apartment, there was no sign of Rita. With the bathroom door open, he could see she wasn't in there.

The front door latch was not engaged and even though Damascus, Oregon, was far from being an unsafe town, he knew Rita always made sure it was latched at night. Chad opened the front door and peered out into the Oregon night sky. He walked down the steps that led to the lower garage area. He stood there for a moment and with both hands grabbed his hair and pushed it towards the back of his head. It began to sink into him that perhaps Rita had left. Then he whispered to himself, "Not perhaps, she has left me."

Chapter 18:
Spider

HEARING THE TAP ON THE WINDOW of his office door, Mayor Harding looked up and through the partially opened blinds to see it was his assistant seeking to come in. He motioned for her to enter with the wave of a hand. His assistant, Shannon Brown, opened the office door and gently shut it behind her as she entered.

Gary Harding leaned back in his leather office chair and pointed for his assistant to take a seat. Shannon complied as she chose one of the two office chairs which faced the mayor's desk. She was holding a stack of papers in her hand and, situating herself comfortably in the chair, placed the papers on her lap and folded both hands on top of the folder that held them. The Mayor smiled at Shannon and spoke, "What can I do for you, Ms. Brown?"

Shannon reciprocated the smile and replied in a professional but firm matter, "Since you passed on any meetings with the Farmer's Co-Op Association to me, because you are just too busy to deal with them, I have just spent the last three hours listening to their bellyaching!"

Gary leaned forward in his chair and with his elbows on his desk, placed his chin on top of his clasped hands. "You know, you sure are pretty when you're perturbed."

Clearly irritated by her boss's playful flirtation, Shannon tossed the folder onto the top of his desk. "Seriously, Gary, these men are making a point to come into the mayor's office once a week and complain that we haven't addressed their request to review the old Johnson property. I'm getting tired of coming up with excuses as to why we keep delaying it."

Tilting his chair, Gary shifted his body to gaze out through his office window that read, in neatly painted gold and black letters:

Gary Harding

Mayor, La Grande, Oregon

His stare was intentional to avoid looking directly at Shannon. After some pondering of her statement, he turned his chair back towards her to answer her. "Geesh, Shannon, I know those guys can be real pains- in-the-you-know-what, but they all accepted and signed the documents allowing their respective farms to annex and purchase partials of Johnson's farm before he died. They all benefited very nicely from that agreement. Simply because the remaining Johnson property is abandoned and the farmhouse has become, well, you know, dilapidated, there isn't much I can do about it."

With a questioning expression on her face, Shannon asked, "What about property taxes? I know Johnson owned the farm, but certainly the county taxes must be delinquent and adding up?"

"That's where the money from the sale of the land parcels goes. Johnson established a Trust from the money he made to pay all taxes, insurance, and any government fees," Harding replied in a matter-of-fact way.

Her eyes stared into his with wonderment. "Must be a heck of a lot of money in that trust to keep paying all these years. But…but why would the old farmer do that?"

"Not sure. It's a mystery to me and everyone else in this county. I guess the law firm that Johnson hired to handle the Trust knows, but they ain't gonna spill the beans. Trust me, I've tried," Gary answered to hopefully end this conversation. It was obvious that Shannon wasn't going to conclude the discussion based on Gary's revelation.

"It just seems like such a shame to let that much quality farmland go untended. The Co-Op is offering to purchase the remaining land from the Trust if the city will condemn the property based on the house being a safety hazard as it is abandoned and in disrepair. They are assuming the gas and electric are still active, and they might be. Just think about the new assessment value of the land once crops were planted. Not to mention the tax revenue from the crops that would be sold," she smugly offered in her stunning commentary.

Gary laughed uncontrollably at her soliloquy. "Maybe you should run for mayor next election. I'd vote for you!"

Shannon stood up and moved to close the blinds that had been partially opened on the office door and the large window. Moving around to where Gary was sitting, she placed one hand on the file she had tossed on his desk a few minutes ago. With her other hand placed open onto Gary's chest, she leaned in to kiss him. Gary did not resist. He knew this visit was not going to end with a passionate kiss. Since he promoted Shannon to be his assistant, she used every asset she encompassed to get her way and today would be no different.

Gary couldn't resist her. Shannon was twenty years his junior and her five-foot eight sculpted body showed the marvel of youth. Her skin was smooth and delicate, and her blonde hair was shoulder length and curled in towards her shoulders. He knew this relationship was wrong. Maybe even illegal, but Shannon was not to be resisted.

As her dark blue dress fell to the ground and Gary stood to embrace her, she whispered in his ear, "This file I brought…"

"Yes," Gary interrupted, and replied as his lips joined hers.

"Maybe we should take a little trip out to Johnson's farm. A little inspection trip, for safety reasons. These are the inspection documents to declare it unsafe and for it to be placed in the control of the city of La Grande," Shannon offered like a black widow spider seducing a mate.

Gary, having been caught in her web like so many times before, replied, "Yes, maybe we should." As their afternoon tryst proceeded, Gary's cell phone began to ring. Looking down at the caller ID illuminated on the phone, Gary turned it over after viewing "Wife calling" on the screen.

Chapter 19:
Falling

HE USED TO HAVE MORALS and protected the integrity that should be displayed by an elected official. Gary Harding was a local boy that had done good by the people of La Grande. He had been the quarterback of the La Grande High School football team that won the first and only Oregon State football championship in the history of the town. He went on to play college football at Oregon State University but despite not being an All American, or even a starter, it paid for his law degree with the scholarship that accompanied being a student athlete.

After passing the bar exam on his first try, he had multiple job offers with law firms across the United States. As much as those offers intrigued Gary, he was resigned to the fact that he was in love with a local La Grande girl. Passing up on the chance to see the world outside the small farming community of La Grande, he settled on marriage to his high school sweetheart, Aspen Simmons, and having a small law practice in town specializing in land sales and various contracts.

Being a local town hero had its rewards and one of those that came to fruition with that fame was to run for, and be elected as, mayor of La Grande. There was a time when everything was perfect. Gary was a respected man in town. He had the power of being mayor. He loved his wife, Aspen, with all his heart. He was the local boy done good. All that changed when Shannon Brown came into his life.

Shannon was introduced to Gary by a colleague as somebody he could rely on to take the stress and strain of his public office and make things easier on him. Gary had no idea that he had that much stress, as the job of being Mayor of La Grande wasn't all that stressful, but he decided to interview Shannon anyway.

When Shannon arrived for the interview, Gary was infatuated with just how attractive she was. He had a hard time not just staring at her like a lustful older man. Even with the way she looked and carried herself, Gary couldn't help but notice she possessed something else. She was smart. Maybe smarter than him. Gary decided no harm could be done having an assistant to help with his day-to-day duties. Plus, she was easy on the eyes. He had no idea that he was hiring a woman that had brains and a body to go with it but also one that would let nothing stand in her way of getting power. The demon inside her made sure of that.

Chapter 20:
Web

She smoothed the wrinkles from her dress that had fallen to the floor during their afternoon meeting. Although nobody else was near when she and Gary completed what they had done so many times before, Shannon scolded Gary to get dressed and comb his hair so nobody might come into his office and be suspicious. Gary complied with her demand. He couldn't resist anything she told him to do.

"Don't forget those inspection documents when we go to Johnson's farm tomorrow morning, my love," Shannon softly and flirtatiously cooed at her boss.

"Maybe we could go to Carver's Inn, get a room for tonight, and leave together in the morning?" Gary replied hoping to continue the events of just a few moments ago.

Smiling at Gary, Shannon brought her open hand to her mouth and blew him a kiss. "Soon, my big handsome boy. We will be together night and day. For now, you need to go home and take care of that wife of yours."

The demon that indwelled Shannon had never used carnal knowledge before in his trade of indwelling. With this host, he was beginning to question why he hadn't.

Gary acknowledged her gesture and puckered his lips and produced a smack resembling a kiss. With that gesture,

Shannon opened Gary's office door and exited into the adjacent office of the mayor. "Ah yes, my wife. I had better call her back or she will question my reason for not picking up her call." Gary had grown tired of Aspen's implications that he might be having an affair. He felt smothered by a woman that had kept him from achieving greatness outside this little hick town of La Grande. She had been good enough for Gary in the beginning of their marriage. Not now though. Ever since Shannon walked through his door.

The phone rang for only a short time before Gary heard Aspen's voice. "Where were you? Why didn't you answer when I called?" Aspen implored.

"Holy Cow, Aspen, I have things to do other than answer the phone at your beck and call!"

Aspen retorted, "I suppose you were in a meeting with Shannon. Seems you are always in a meeting with Shannon."

Gary rolled his eyes as he replied to his wife's usual questioning of Gary's fidelity. "As a matter of fact, I was in a meeting with Shannon. She just completed a grueling three-hour session with the Farmer's Co-Op. We're going to inspect Johnson's farm tomorrow morning. There is a concern about the condition of the house."

"So, are you going to need to pull another all-nighter to prepare for this important inspection?" Aspen blurted out like a prosecuting attorney questioning a defendant on the stand.

Gary had grown tired of this conversation. Wanting to end it and have his mind return to the bliss he encountered earlier in the arms of Shannon, he shut down his wife's inquisition. "Aspen, nothing is going on between me and Shannon. You're just imagining things. I'll be home shortly. Maybe we can go out for dinner at the golf course. You would like that, wouldn't you?" The call ended with Aspen pleading for her husband to honor his offer and come home.

At home, Shannon kicked off her high heeled shoes and pulled off her work dress. She walked to the kitchen with only her undergarments on and pulled a bottle of Vodka from an open cabinet and poured a half glass of the vodka over some ice she had dispensed from the refrigerator. Curling up on the sofa, with one leg tucked up and beneath her rear end, she drank the entire contents before crushing one of the ice cubes between her teeth.

"Good job today. You have served me well and for this I cherish you. Soon, the mortal will worship you and you will have complete power over him. Just as I do over you!" The voice in her head rang with the voice of a thousand souls that had come before her.

Chapter 21:
The Cave

HE HAD NO SANCTUARY AND NEVER DESIRED ONE. Orin
retreated to a small cave surrounded by boulders and small
shrubs. He desired no mortal comfort or pleasures of this
earthly domain. He was an angel of the legion of Lucifer.
That was enough and should be enough for any demon.
Human sanctuaries disgusted him along with the demons
that utilized these mortal habitats. "Yes, this will do just
fine. These dark and damp walls would not be appropriate
for any mortal or demon," Orin thought with full
repulsiveness for both.

A stalactite caressed his cheek despite him not
appearing as a mortal in this place. Orin's spiritual
manifestation needn't worry about these obstacles in this
cave, but he did admire the way this earthly formation
pushed towards the ground. With the passing years it
continued its journey toward his home. The home he
desired to return to but knew it would be a long time in
earthly years before that happened.

In this place he began to ponder his plan to indwell the
offspring of Dante. Perhaps it was not the right time to
proceed. Not in the sanctuary that the infant currently lived
its dependent existence on Dante and his mate. "Maybe

Ignis was wise in his declaration for me to not underestimate the mortal, Dante. Patience is my plan. Let Dante leave this domicile. It might have special protection from Gabriel or…" Orin shuddered at his thought that the Archangel Michael might be giving Dante protection. "Yes, I will follow Dante to his new sanctuary. He would not suspect that the angels of Lucifer could or would pursue him. He would be vulnerable to a cunning angel such as myself. Yes, patience, that is my plan!"

Outside of Orin's ability to perceive or recognize the existence of any other company in the dark and stark habitat of the cave, a mighty creation of the God of the universe stood, watching, as the vile demon plotted against Dante.

Chapter 22:
No Entrance

WHEN GARY HARDING WALKED INTO THE HOUSE, he experienced anxiety in anticipation of the continued wrath he would receive from his wife. He knew he probably deserved all of it, but he also knew he was a weak man. A man that could not resist the temptations offered by Shannon Brown.

Aspen held back the wrath that Gary anticipated. This surprised him, and the conversation between them as they dined at the golf course restaurant was infrequent and consisted of superficial chit-chat. When the couple resigned their day to go to bed, Aspen reached across the bed to touch her husband on the shoulder. Gary understood why she had made that gesture, but he just couldn't reciprocate. His desire to be intimate with Aspen had left many months ago. He had found another to satisfy those needs and, in those arms, had begun a departure from the vows he shared with God and the woman who was in his bed.

The next morning Gary brought his truck to a stop in front of the mayor's office. Placing the transmission into park, he waved at Shannon as she exited her car and walked towards his truck. Reaching across the cab, he grabbed the inside door handle to swing it open for her to enter. She struggled to get the door open due to having two Styrofoam cups filled with coffee to enjoy on their journey to Johnson's farm.

"Always thinking of me, aren't you, Shannon?" Reaching to accept his cup, Gary smiled like a worker getting his paycheck on payday. Shannon handed it to him as she climbed into the cab of the truck.

She settled into her seat and reached to put on her seatbelt. "Did you remember the County inspection documents?"

Gary replied sarcastically, "Well, good morning to you, too. Yes, they are in my briefcase behind my seat."

"Sorry, honey. I'm just anxious to get on our way so we can get this done and take over Johnson's farm. Good morning, my love," Shannon responded while reaching across the cab to kiss him on the cheek.

Gary quickly glanced around the surroundings of the street to insure nobody had witnessed Shannon's display of affection. He returned his gaze towards Shannon who looked magnificent in tight blue jeans that were tucked into cowboy boots. She wore a white V-neck t shirt underneath a plaid shirt tucked into the front of her jeans. She was a knockout that his wife Aspen could not hold a candle to. Gary placed the truck into drive and pulled out onto Main Street heading northeast towards Johnson's farm.

It was late September in La Grande and the approaching fall was bringing its changes upon the landscape. As various farms rolled by, showing the effects of a completed harvest of various crops, Gary and Shannon talked of their plans. Plans of Gary's professional future and how Shannon fit into all of it.

Gary, in thoughtful reflection, spoke out as he drove on the dirt roadway that was common in these parts, adorned with an occasional farmhouse with land and livestock, "I'm thinking about running for Governor."

"Really?" Shannon replied showing a false curiosity. It had always been her plan for Gary to do so. She had just bided her time for him to come to the decision himself, so she didn't come across as too pushy. "I think you would be a great Governor. Where do I fit into those plans?"

Gary laughed at Shannon's response. "I wouldn't run without you by my side."

Shannon responded with a sense of sarcasm, "Which side? The one opposite of your wife?"

"Aspen won't be with me. She's content to be a local girl. She holds me back. If she was the mayor's wife for the next forty years that would be just fine with her. But not for me," Gary responded like a patient on a psychiatrist's couch.

Shannon did not provide a response to Gary's proclamation. Instead, she turned her head towards the passenger side window and secretly smiled. She watched the dirt and dust swirl about the truck as they proceeded along the rural road and thought to herself just how far she had come in her journey for power.

She had no clue how she had achieved this standing. Intuition, maybe? A long time ago a voice in her head told her that she was smart. When nobody else would-parents, teachers, family- her esteem plummeted, and she felt less than everybody. Shannon had no friends growing up. Nobody to confide in about her feelings and her parents were too busy in their careers to care.

Then, when Shannon turned sixteen, she heard the voice and the voice explained to her how to use the power of being smart. Where there were once no friends, nobody to care, suddenly, all the boys in school started to pay attention. It was the voice that told her how to use the boys. To get love, but mostly, to get what she wanted. She has used that power ever since. Now, when she uses that power, everybody thinks she's a genius. Especially Gary.

"Here we are!" Gary blurted out. The road that paralleled Johnson's farm ran along a barbed wire fence that had seen better days. The truck vibrated along as the road was wash boarded and rough. Gary could see the entrance that led to the old and tired farmhouse. A wrought iron gate with a rusty chain wrapped around a rough and splintered wood post was the obstacle to proceed to the front of the farmhouse.

Standing in front of the gate was Myron Hastings, one of the Co-Op members who had purchased adjacent land from Johnson.

Climbing out of the cab of his truck, Gary responded to Hastings unexpected appearance, "I didn't expect anybody to be here today, Myron."

"Ms. Brown informed us that you were eager to inspect this place. We're all eager for the same thing. Just look at this place! Weeds have overgrown everything, and Johnson's house looks like it could fall, or burn down any minute," Hastings responded with the angst of a trip to the dentist.

Gary looked over at Shannon, who had also gotten out of the truck, with disdain in his eyes, being a bit perturbed that she would have told anybody about them coming today. She didn't return the stare, but simply continued to look forward towards the farmhouse.

The look on Shannon's face was disconcerting to Gary. It was almost like she was in a trance. Her gaze could not be interrupted despite Gary calling out her name several times.

"Plus, I think we might have a squatter," Hastings proclaimed.

Gary returned his attention to Hastings and asked, "What makes you think so, Myron?"

Myron Hastings pointed toward the front porch of the farmhouse. "Right there. It's a jar on the front step. Looks like it's got tea in it. Fresh tea!"

Chapter 23:
1987

MINUTES TURNED INTO HOURS, and hours into days and months. At first Chad figured that Rita would return to him and their little apartment. She would admit that the solitude she had been experiencing, and that was causing her so much distress, was not Chad's fault or problem, and she would beg him to come home. After so much time had passed with no word from Rita, he finally resigned himself that she was gone.

The cell phone rang showing the number calling was from Jensen's Automotive. Chad reluctantly answered the call. The voice on the other end of the call was the owner, Mack Jensen. "Hey, Perryman, you gonna come to work today? These cars ain't gonna fix themselves and I need you here!"

Chad knew he had extended the patience of his boss far beyond limits. "I know, boss. I just haven't felt well enough to come to work. I need a few more days off and then I'll be fine," Chad's voice emitted a lack of honesty.

"Look, kid, we've all had women problems. Can't live with em, and you can't hunt em!" Mack Jensen chuckled, hoping his insensitive joking would diffuse the uncomfortable conversation he was having with his prized mechanic.

Chad did not acknowledge his bosses attempt at jovial humor. "I'll be there Monday morning, Mack."

With that statement Jensen forced a reply to end the conversation that he thought he would never have to make. "Well, ya better be here kid or ya better move on to something else."

Chad placed the receiver on the cradle of the rotary-dial phone to end the call and rolled over on the bed reaching for the spot where Rita used to lie. A tear rolled down Chad's cheek. Tears had once been foreign to him but now it seemed that, as he continued to plummet into the despair of depression, they were common companions to his existence.

Sleep was the only bastion of peace that Chad had to combat his deep depression. Rita had helped to squelch the effects that the disease caused. Chad didn't understand nor acknowledge that depression had always been the source of his quietness, but with Rita by his side, he combatted its controlling effects. Rolling out of his latest bout of sleep, Chad moved slowly to the shower. "I must get out of this apartment. I need to get some air," Chad thought to himself as the hot water created steam engulfing his body.

Slipping on his black motorcycle jacket, Chad exited the apartment and made his way down the stairs. Below his apartment was the garage that housed his motorcycle. The only thing in Chad's orbit of life that brought him pleasure. He ran his hand over the gas tank which held the decal, Rita. He had often thought of removing the decal from his bike, but he just couldn't bring himself to do it. He lifted his leg over the seat and with one upward lift with the heel of his boot, the kickstand moved upward. The engine rumbled and Chad released the clutch to begin his journey to anywhere but here. It was time to ride and the Northwest roads ahead of him held some peace he so desperately sought.

Chad had been a half an hour into his aimless ride when he realized old habits had led to the road that held the biker's tavern that he often frequented along the Clackamas River. Not really wanting social interaction, Chad reluctantly turned his bike into the tavern parking lot.

The tavern did not appear crowded so he figured he might be able to stop, have a beer, and at least be amongst other human beings that did not carry the weight of his sorrows. At least this place was familiar. Deep down, Chad couldn't discount that he really wanted to be surrounded by the sights and smells of the first place he met Rita.

Chad entered the tavern and walked up to the bar area and quietly took a stool. The bartender recognized him and quickly moved to address him. "Hey, Chad. Long time, no see."

Chad gave the bartender a reluctant smile and replied, "Yah, it's been a while. I've been purty busy. I'll have whatever you got on tap."

The bartender acknowledged Chad's request and grabbed a glass to begin the pour of a local brew. Chad glanced around the bar area and was grateful he did not recognize anybody. The bartender placed Chad's beer in front of him and Chad wiped the excess beer from the lacquered bar top that had fallen down the side of the glass. He was content to not make eye contact with anybody else sitting at the bar and quietly drank his beer.

Chad finished his beer and placed money on the bar. As he was preparing to depart the bar stool and exit the tavern, Chad felt a soft hand touch his left shoulder. He quickly spun to see the owner of the hand that had been placed on his shoulder and he was stunned beyond comprehension. Standing to his left was Rita, with a subtle smile on her face.

"Hi, Chad. I'm surprised, but glad, to see you here." Rita spoke, but Chad heard nothing of what she had just said.

Chad was tongue tied and unable to respond to her.

"Just like normal, not much to say," Rita tried not to make her statement sound sarcastic.

Chad could do the only thing his emotions and reflexes could muster; he grabbed Rita and gave her a hug that lifted her feet from the bar floor. Putting her down, Chad produced a guarded laugh but the look on his face displayed great relief and joy. "I've missed you so much, Rita. You have no idea just how much I've missed you!" Just as soon as these words came out of Chad's mouth, a well-built biker with a black tee shirt that was probably two sizes too small, in order to display his obvious muscular build, stepped in front of Rita and placed both hands on the collar of Chad's black motorcycle jacket. "Hey, dude! You better be careful whose woman you hug like a bear!" Impatience and anger were evident in the voice of Chad's attacker.

Chad was surprised and taken back by the man's statement. He glanced around the man's hulking body to try and glimpse the expression on Rita's face. "She is…was…my woman, butthead!" Chad responded in a clearly agitated way.

Not expecting this moment to turn violent, Chad soon found himself on the barroom floor. A quick right fist had landed on Chad's cheek, forcing him to lose consciousness for a short moment. Stunned, but angered enough to reciprocate, Chad and his attacker found themselves being abruptly escorted from the bar area and out the front door of the tavern. Both men stumbled with the force of their exit from the tavern and spilled out into the parking lot.

Gayland hovered in the background, sensing this was a soul worth the taking. He was usually more diligent in his selections, but this mortal intrigued him in so many ways.

He wasn't particularly prone to choose bikers as mortals to indwell. They were too volatile.   Maybe it was his physique. He did remind him of the great Demetri's physical appearance, but Gayland didn't want to be accused by other demons of copying Demetri. He realized just then, right before the moment he took Chad, it was the mortal's jacket. He realized then, "It is divine."

Chad jumped to his feet with full expectations of his attacker wishing to continue the confrontation and was quickly rewarded for his intuition. The man approached Chad and bent at his waist to tackle and gain control of Chad on the ground. Despite the black shirted man being of a muscular build, it was obvious to Chad that this person had too much to drink. Even with the advantage of Chad only having one beer, he didn't want to hurt this man. Despite this man being a physical specimen, Chad was a fighter, and he knew that even without alcohol involved, he could hurt the man. Unfortunately, the man was relentless and continued to pursue the fight.

Rita had come outside and tried to break up the fight that was occurring between the men. Chad tried his best to honor her wishes. He did his best until his attacker produced a knife in his right hand. A fast slash to Chad's left arm alerted him to the appearance of the knife. Luckily, none of Chad's flesh had been touched but a gash in the black leather jacket had been opened.

"I'm gonna kill you…you son of a bitch!" The stranger bellowed like a blast furnace at Chad. With both men now postured in front of each other, and tavern patrons spilling out to witness the event, Rita rushed towards the black shirted man, attempting to calm him down. Her efforts were not well received, and, with the back of his hand, the man landed a blow that sent Rita reeling to the ground.

Like a man possessed, Chad lost all control of his reality and senses. The next thing he knew, Rita was pulling him off the stranger. He snapped out of his trance and recognized that the man had succumbed to several of his angered blows. Feeling his senses return to him, Chad looked at Rita's somber, pleading face, then his glance turned towards the bloodied face of the man who had slashed his beloved leather jacket. He did not recognize the man. His blows had been quite fierce and extensive.

Rita scrambled past Chad to reach the man lying unconscious on the dirt ground. She placed herself over his limp body and with his blood having rubbed onto Rita's cheek, she turned her tear-stained face back to look at Chad. Screaming like a crazed person at the man she once loved, Rita yelled out to Chad, "You could have killed him! You could have killed my husband!"

Chapter 24:
Journey

ALEX GLANCED AROUND THE MODEST HOUSE that had been his home since arriving in the coastal city of Astoria. This had been the place of many miraculous events. His late-night rendezvous with the Angel, Gabriel, and his Lord and Savior. He couldn't help but also recall his meeting with the demon, Demetri. So many life changing events had happened in this home, but none bigger than sharing it with his beautiful wife, Courtney.

Reaching from behind, Courtney placed her hands around Alex's chest in a tender hug, "Reminiscing, my love?"

Alex let out a big sigh as he turned to face Courtney. Holding her in his arms while looking into her eyes, he answered her question. "Yep, not all my memories are good, but most of them are fantastic."

Courtney smiled as she responded with a question, "Are we doing the right thing?"

Alex looked at her with all the reassurance of a General leading his superior fighting force into battle,

"Beats me! I have no idea if we're doing the right thing but, it's too late now. The U-Haul is all loaded, and the car's packed with our clothes so…"

Once again, humor was injected into their conversation to diffuse the anxiety of the moment. Courtney responded with the remnant of chuckling still present. "I've checked everything. All the motel reservations for our trip to Colorado have been made, so we can load up and begin our new journey. You, me, and Annie."

Alex took one last glance around his living room, half expecting George to appear with a smile and wink, but, it didn't happen. "I hate that you and Annabel will be alone in the car this whole trip while I drive the U-Haul. If Annie gets fussy, just pull over and I'll follow," Alex instructed.

"Oh, I will. Lucky we aren't under any time pressure. I'm not sure how she'll do on a long road trip." Courtney affirmed.

Alex and Courtney walked out of the front door with Annabel. After placing Annabel in her car seat and ensuring she was comfortable and content, for the moment, Courtney kissed Alex and crawled into the overstuffed car. Alex motioned for Courtney to roll down the car window. Leaning into the window, Alex gave a big kiss to her. "I'm following you all the way to Tyler and Cindy's house so you're in the lead," Alex offered control to her as any good subordinate would.

"What if I can't remember how to get to their house? They were so kind to let us spend the night before our cross-country trek. You've placed a lot of faith in me," Courtney replied while trying to suppress the sarcasm.

Alex got a serious look on his face as he pondered his answer. "Well, we have a blow-up mattress in the U-Haul. I guess we'll just have to sleep in the woods tonight."

Alex and Courtney laughed and winked at each other as Alex made his way back to crawl into the cab of the U-Haul, start the truck engine, and begin the journey to Colorado. As he placed the transmission into drive, he looked to his right to see the Pacific Ocean as it accepted the infusion of water from the Columbia River. Most of his whole life had existed on this sandy but rocky coast of Oregon. He sensed he would miss it.

Courtney took one quick glance back at Annie who was still preoccupied with the rattle that had been placed into her tiny hand. She saw her husband wave at her from the cab of the U-Haul as she pulled down the street. "I guess we really are doing this," she whispered to herself as the distance from their Astoria bungalow proved to eclipse any vision of it from her sight.

With the excitement of the journey ahead of them, both Courtney and Annabel were oblivious to an unseen passenger who was riding in the backseat. Hidden amongst the blankets and pillows they had used as bedding was a spirit. An evil spirit that had decided to ride with his future target. A target that would bring the many answers that his master desired, and with those answers, fame, and power that even the reviled Demetri had never known.

Chapter 25:
Entrance

Shannon was pale. Gary became alarmed since this was not the skin tone he was used to seeing in her complexion. "Shannon! Shannon! What's wrong? Say something, please!" Gary implored, hoping to gain her attention and bring her focus back onto him. Suddenly, Shannon's eyes rolled toward the top of her eyelids, her knees buckled beneath her, and she fainted to the ground.

Gary ran to where Shannon had collapsed. Dropping to his knees, he was confused on what to do to help her. This confusion intensified as Shannon's body began to convulse. Turning to look at Myron Hastings, Gary called out to him in a panicked manner, "Call 911! Call 911, now!" Myron, who was stupefied, was slow to react to Gary's command.

"We got no cellphone coverage out here!" Myron responded to Gary's demand holding up his phone in one hand and pointing at it with the other. Gary whose attention was now focused on bringing aid to Shannon's uncontrollable twitching, screamed in anger at Myron, "You don't need coverage, you moron! A 911 call will go through!"

Hastings acknowledged Gary's revelation and fumbled to hit the digits on his phone that would bring help. A 911 dispatcher answered the call. "This is a 911 dispatcher. What is the nature of your emergency?"

"Uhm, this is Myron Hastings. I'm at the old Johnson farm with Mayor Harding. His assistant, Shannon Brown, passed out and she's shaking."

The dispatcher inquired in a calm and concise manner, "Is she having a seizure?"

"I don't know what that is." Myron replied.

"Is she conscious and breathing?"

Myron looked at Gary who was now laying behind Shannon attempting to calm her convulsions. "Is she breathing, Harding?"

Frantically, Gary called out, "Yes, she's breathing. Tell them to get an ambulance out here immediately!"

After several interchanges with Hastings working as the communication intermediary between the 911 dispatcher and Gary, he hung up the phone. "They'll have an ambulance here soon, Gary," Hastings informed the mayor in what seemed like a perturbed manner at being put into the position of having to make the call.

In that moment, Gary witnessed Shannon's seizure subside and her eyes return to stare vacantly at him. "Shannon, my dear Shannon, are you okay? Lay still, an ambulance is on its way. You're going to be alright," Gary pleaded with her in hopes his words would ring true.

What happened next brought both Hastings and Gary to the brink of understanding exactly what they were witnessing. A voice emitted from Shannon's mouth. It was a voice that was not Shannon's. It was deep and rough. With a deeply guttural echo. It was male without mistake. "We cannot pass. The pain… the pain…"

Gary looked up at Myron Hastings wondering if he had heard the same words being formed from Shannon's voice. "What pain, Shannon? Where does it hurt?" Gary implored of Shannon whose eyes were still wide open, but vacant. No additional words came from Shannon's mouth. Her eyes closed as the ambulance, with sirens blaring, approached Gary, Shannon, and Hastings, who were postured just at the edge of Johnson's farm entrance.

On the front porch of the farmhouse, standing near the top step, stood a demon, holding a feral cat in his demon arms. Taking in the entirety of the events that had unfolded just outside the gate that marked the entrance to his farm, he understood what had just occurred. Placing the cat down and onto the porch, he retired to his rocking chair. Picking up the glass of iced tea that sat by his chair, he drank.

Chapter 26:
Delivered

With blood on his hurting hands, Chad stood to his feet. He had lost all humanity when he had pummeled the stranger who knocked his beloved Rita to the ground. Every punch he landed to tear the flesh and crunch the bone on the man that Rita now hovered over paled in comparison to the blow Rita had landed on him.

"Husband?" Chad's voice quivered to speak the words.

Rita turned away from the man on the ground and stood to face Chad. "He is my husband, Chad!" With tears and mascara streaming from her eyes and down her cheeks, Rita drove piercing words into Chad's flesh. "I loved you, Chad. I just couldn't stay with you. You couldn't understand that all I ever needed was you. Just you. You left me long before I ever left you!"

Chad absorbed Rita's words the best a wounded man could. Gayland reveled in the hurt his host was feeling. It was a desperate hurt. The type of hurt that would cause poor decisions to be made. Sirens wailed in the distance and Chad knew he would be the object of interest when the police arrived. "Not what you want tonight. To be arrested and spend your freedom in jail," Gayland subtly whispered into Chad's conscious.

Stumbling to his precious Harley Softail motorcycle, Chad glanced back at Rita. He yearned for her. He wished she would run to his bike, jump on the back, and ride off with him. Chad realized that was a dream that would never come true. For some reason, which he couldn't acknowledge where the feeling came from, Chad felt a twinge of hatred for Rita. Hatred such as he had never felt before. He started his bike and put it into gear. As he drove down the twisting turns away from the tavern, Chad looked back to see the flashing lights of law enforcement pulling into the parking lot of the tavern. He accelerated to put as much distance as he could between him and, for tonight, the loss of freedom that he faced.

Gayland was exhilarated. The wind blowing through the hair of his indwelled subject was a sensation he had never experienced before. He wondered just how long he would be with this mortal before his soul was eventually delivered to his master.

After approximately 30 minutes had passed and Chad saw no signs of pursuit from the police, he pulled his bike over to the side of the road. Climbing off the seat, but still sitting sideways, Chad felt the tear in his jacket. He stretched to relieve the pain that existed in his lower back. Most likely caused by the fight. His jaw was sore from the punch Rita's husband had delivered and his heart ached from the punches she had delivered to his soul.

He knew he couldn't go home. The police would be waiting for him there. Basically, his life was over. He would lose his job, his beloved bike, and now, he had lost Rita. Tears streamed down Chad Perryman's face. Swinging his leg back over the seat of the motorcycle, Chad hit the ignition and gazed out into the Oregon sky. The moon was full, not absorbed by the usual Northwest cloud cover, and Chad sighed.

The Douglas fir trees glistened in the moonlight and Chad could see that the road he was traveling upon was elevated above the forest below.

Gayland was intrigued by what would come next with this mortal. He didn't try and influence his host. Gayland decided to just sit back and experience the ride. So, to speak.

As the 1986 Harley Softail was put into gear, Gayland felt Chad accelerating fast. The speed picked up with each shift of the gears, and soon the bike was travelling much faster than the road could accommodate. Gayland could feel the moisture of the fluid that was secreted from Chad's eyes. He could not feel how moist they were, nor if they were hot or cold, salty or fresh.

The front tire of the motorcycle continued to spin after leaving the pavement and going airborne. Gayland felt the body of Chad being hurtled forward, no longer attached to the motorcycle. As Chad's body hit the top of a tree, Gayland knew his time with this host was over. It saddened him, he assumed it was because he had spent so little time with this host, but the sadness only lasted for a moment.

Deep down a crevice of the forest that served to let water runoff careen down its landscape, Chad's lifeless body laid amongst the dirt, rock, and ferns. The broken appendages intrigued Gayland. He could sense, in this mortal state, that Chad's arms and legs were not positioned where they would normally be on a human body. Chad's face was disfigured, and blood and torn skin dominated the skull they once adorned. Gayland hovered above the mortal's body. Waiting and watching for his master to arrive.

"This soul was captured for me, much faster than you expected, wasn't it, my dear Gayland?"

"Yes, master. Sooner is good, sometimes," Gayland answered with the acknowledgement that his master had arrived.

Lucifer hovered around the lifeless body of Chad Perryman. Surveying the remnant of a once living human being, Gayland watched as his lord and master waited for the soul of the human to appear before him. Suddenly, the spirit of Chad Perryman rose from the carnage that was displayed on the forest floor and stood before Gayland and Satan.

Lucifer spoke to the apparition as a father would to a disobedient offspring. "So, you have stood before the one that claims to be God of the Universe and have been found to be unworthy. Now, you come to me, your true god, the rightful lord, to decide your eternity."

The spirit that once was the mortal, Chad Perryman, began to writhe in pain. Gayland had seen this before and knew what was coming.

A portal opened near where the body of Chad was laying. From the portal came screams of torture and anguish. Devoid of any hope or happiness. The soul of Chad Perryman was thrown into the portal like a rag doll falling from a child's arms.

As the portal was closing, Gayland could see a sinister smile form on the spirit face of his master. Gayland could not help but notice how unbecoming the smile was on the face of his master. Especially since the triumph over Gabriel's God was an eternity of pain and suffering for one Chad Perryman.

Lucifer summoned Gayland before him, to which he obeyed without question. He peered into the mind of his servant, Gayland. "You covet the jacket that the mortal wore, don't you?"

"I do not covet human things, my lord," Gayland replied with as much assurance as he could muster.

Lucifer laughed. "It is allowed, my dear Gayland, if it comes from yours truly."

Gayland was confused as to how to respond to his master. With a bewildered look on his demon face,

Gayland peered down at his spirit and began to witness the forming of a mortal physique. Coming to fruition was the object of his demon desire. His mortal form was that of Chad Perryman. Leather jacket and all.

"Time for you to take on your mortal persona, my faithful servant. You coveted this human's look and now, as my gift to you, you have it." Satan smugly replied.

Gayland caressed the leather jacket with his mortal hands and spoke, "You are my lord and in this I am greatly pleased."

Gayland noticed that the leather jacket was still attached to the broken body of Chad Perryman. He understood this was just a replica that adorned his physical manifestation. Still, it was magnificent.

"Now, go to your sanctuary, my faithful servant. Enjoy your time at my farm which I have provided for you. In time, I will summon you, and other members of my legion, to perform a service for me. I have sensed that the God of Gabriel plots against me. I will need my legion to root out that plot," Lucifer commanded.

With those words spoken by his master, Gayland was standing on the porch of the house on Johnson's farm. He was pleased to be back on the farm. Gayland was also grateful that delivering the soul of Chad Perryman was swift and his master adorned him with the gift of the mortal's jacket.

Just then, words that were spoken to him, by Lucifer, surfaced with an air of blasphemy. 'Enjoy your time at my farm.' These words brought a slight twinge of anger to the demon's mind. "This is my farm! It was given to me by the farmer and his wife. I am the rightful owner," he proclaimed over and over in his demon mind.

Chapter 27:
Farewell

CINDY MCINTYRE STRUGGLED TO LET GO OF COURTNEY. Alex reveled in the length of time the embrace between the two women lasted. He wasn't about to signal an end to the hug. Cindy had been such a pivotal part of his journey into understanding his mission for God and he cherished the moments their two families could share. Those moments were about to become less frequent due to this being the last stop the Dante's would make before they began their journey to Colorado.

"I really appreciate that you and Alex have decided to just give Annabel to Tyler and me," Cindy joked as tears of loss streamed down her face.

Courtney reciprocated the joke and replied, "Sure, no problem. We're tired of her anyway!"

Annabel slept comfortably in her car seat knowing that she was loved and meant everything to her parents.

Alex embraced Tyler with the affection of two brothers, two brothers in the faith, that battle against evil. Tyler slapped Alex on each of his shoulders. "If there's anything we can help you with, Alex, please don't hesitate to call us," Tyler offered in sincere hope that his friend would take him up on the offer.

"You know that I appreciate you, my friend. You and Cindy know you must come and visit Court and me when we get settled in Colorado."

Tyler shrugged his shoulders and replied, "Maybe. You guys are such a bad influence on my wife. All she talks about is having a baby!"

Alex chuckled at that statement by his friend. "Well then, I'm glad we're such a poor influence on Cindy." Alex gleamed a smile at Tyler that showed it was time to depart on their journey. As Alex climbed into the cab of the truck, he stopped suddenly. "Come to think of it, Tyler, I do have a favor you can do for me. If you're willing."

Tyler moved closer to the cab of the U-Haul and responded, "Anything, Alex. Just name it."

"My favor involves demons," Alex offered.

Tyler was intrigued and invigorated by what his friend had just said. Alex's journey with the forces of evil and the spirit world had always been something that he was curious about and studied in his Christian learning.

"Me? Demons? Alex, I don't have the same abilities, or anointing from God that you have. How could I help you with demons?"

Alex smiled a broad smile and answered his friend. "Stay out of the way of this demon. It's Gayland. I need you to go to his sanctuary farm. It's in La Grande. He'll need help, soon. Human help. I know you're very busy with the Church, and this is asking a lot, but you are somebody I can trust."

With wonderment etched all over his face, Tyler replied, "Will I be able to see Gayland? Will he be able to speak to me?"

"No. He'll be curious as to why you're there but will soon discover you're there because I sent you. All I ask is that you be careful with his iced tea."

"Iced tea?" Tyler questioned.

"Don't try and make sense of it now, Tyler. Someday I'll explain it to you. Can I count on you to do me this favor? It'll be fine if you want to take Cindy with you. Gayland will be aware of who she is. He'll behave in total reverence to the girl who helped defeat the mighty Demetri."

"I said I would do anything to help, Alex, and I meant it. What do you need me to do when we get there?

"There's a new refrigerator being delivered. Just let the delivery man in and make sure he sets it up correctly. Oh yah, make sure you get the old ice cube trays out of the old refrigerator before they haul it off."

"Old ice trays. Got it. When do we need to be at the farm?" Tyler inquired.

"The new refrigerator's being delivered between 1 o'clock and 4 o'clock on Tuesday," Alex answered.

"What would you've done if Cindy and me couldn't make it?"

Alex bellowed a big laugh and replied, "That never entered my mind."

Alex closed the door of the cab and simultaneously yelled out at Tyler, "I love you, buddy!"

Chapter 28:
Orin's Trail

THE DANTE'S CONVOY TURNED ONTO I-84. Courtney felt a twinge of remorse as she viewed the magnificence of Multnomah Falls just to the south. She wondered if Alex was also enjoying the scenery before them. As they headed east towards The Dalles, the Columbia River began to display its power as it carved out the wonders of the Gorge. This would be the last time, for quite a while, that the splendors of the Northwest would be available for her to enjoy.

She was excited about Colorado. Her senses revealed that with all the beauty she had experienced growing up in Oregon, Colorado would offer equal places. Annabel would always know where she was born, Courtney would make sure of that, but Annie's earliest memories would be of the beauty and majesty of her Colorado home.

Orin was fascinated by the young human that he shared the backseat with. From time to time, he would dabble with making himself known to Annabel, but, at the same time, not risk exposing himself to the mate of Dante who commanded this carriage in which they traveled. The demon was astonished, but at the same time concerned, that the young mortal could sense he was there. Each time he tried to be more curious about any power she might be endowed with, the infant began to cry. "Perhaps she is beginning to have the same ability to see magnificent angels as her sire," Orin pondered.

After a couple of attempts, Orin decided it was best to leave the confines of traveling with these female mortals or otherwise risk being detected. Orin had never dealt with the possibility of indwelling a human this young. It was all uncharted territory for him. Instead, Orin hovered above the Dante's. He stayed close enough to track them without the mortal Alex Dante being able to spot his presence. He needed to know exactly where these mortals were at every moment.

Plus, he could no longer stand the music that was engulfing the carriage. The music echoed the glories of Gabriel's God with each repetitive note. This music repulsed him, just like the host of Angels singing and worshipping the false God of Gabriel. This way he wouldn't have to listen to the mysterious singing of the glories of God inside the travelling coach.

With the majesty of the Columbia River behind their caravan, Alex began to see the mileage marker signs noting the distance to La Grande. Eastern Oregon provided different scenery. Forested terrain began to yield to pastures and the promise of flat, fertile farmland. He also knew that just outside of La Grande, there existed a farm unlike any other.

A farm that had long since seen its growing season and harvest pass. Now all that existed at this once producing farm was a single demon. The same demon that had tracked him since his youth to provide his former master information about him. This demon, despite no hope for a glorious eternity, was a traitor to the same master that entrusted him. Gayland now existed to serve Alex. Alex knew he was using Gayland. He was using the demon to distract and confuse the evil one.

This did not cause distress to Alex. He felt it was payback for the years that Gayland had used him. George, who transfigured to be the Angel Gabriel, often coached Alex to not feel remorse for any defeated demon. He reminded Alex that all demons had made their beds and now must lay in them.

Alex picked up his cell phone and called Courtney's number. She answered her phone in a jovial manner, "Dante's moving company. How may I direct your call?'

"I'd like to complain to the manager, please," Alex returned the humor.

"Well, she is currently asleep in the back seat, but I can have her return your call when she awakes."

Alex chuckled, "Never mind. You sound cute. I'd rather talk to you."

"I'm not really. I'm actually quite hideous, but I'll let you buy me some gas," Courtney replied.

Alex looked at his gas gauge and decided that, despite having ulterior motives for stopping in La Grande, he could also use a fill up. "I was thinking we would stop for gas in La Grande and have lunch."

"Good idea. I'm a little hungry," Courtney issued her approval of Alex's suggestion.

"Courtney, just so you know, I have another reason for stopping in La Grande. After lunch I need to have a few minutes to visit somebody."

Courtney quickly developed a concerned look on her face after hearing this newest revelation from Alex. "Is this visit demon related, my husband?"

"In a way. Except I won't be seeing a demon. I need to visit with a lawyer in town."

Courtney responded, "You're always a mystery, my love. I assume this isn't a divorce lawyer?"

"Never! You make too much money now for me to leave," Alex quipped.

The couple shared a much-needed laugh and hung up their respective phones. As Alex led the way into the business center of La Grande, he stopped at a local gas station and proceeded to fill up their vehicles. Courtney motioned at Alex and pointed across the street from the gas station. "That looks like a nice diner. Should we just eat there?"

"Perfect. I need to get my bearings on where the law office is."

The family enjoyed a nice lunch devoid of the pressures of the road. Annabel enjoyed her baby food although her face would not indicate any of the food made its way to her stomach. The waitress cleared the dishes from the Dante's table and handed them the lunch check. Alex stopped the waitress and inquired, "Would you happen to know where the law offices of Turner, Gill and Makowski are located?"

The waitress pointed just west of the diner. "Sure, they're just two blocks straight west of here. Can't miss them. They're on the north side of the street."

As Alex opened the car door for Courtney and Annie, Courtney asked, "You won't be too long, will you? I'm going to feed Annie here in the car. I'm sure she'll fall asleep, but I think we need to get back on the road. We have motel reservations tonight and I don't want to arrive too late."

"No worries, Court. I'll make it quick."

Alex decided it was easier to walk down to the lawyer's office than try to park the U-Haul, so he briskly set off down Main Street. After a short while, Alex arrived at his destination. He was expecting a more professional facade than what he found. This law firm received the highest grades possible from its constituents when he read the online reviews, but they certainly didn't sink any of the money they earned into their building. "Perhaps being frugal is a good thing," Alex pondered as he opened the front door to enter.

The interior office matched the element of no pomp or circumstance that the exterior displayed. "Well, at least they're consistent," Alex decided. The front office offered no receptionist to greet him and Alex wondered if he might have stumbled in during their lunch hour. Just as Alex strode towards an open office door to see if any soul might exist in this office, a tall older man with a large white cowboy hat came walking out of the very same office where Alex was heading.

The man under the hat smiled a broad smile at Alex and extended his right arm and hand. "Good afternoon, sir. I'm Jim Turner. Many apologies for not hearing you come in. What can I do for you today?"

Alex studied the kindly older gentleman. He admired the lines and wrinkles on his face. The darker skin on his arms revealed he was more than a lawyer. This was a man that did more than just sit behind a desk or walk the short distance to the courthouse. This was a man that also worked the land. Alex returned the man's smile and shook his hand. "Hello, I'm Alex Dante. I'm on the Trust for the Johnson property."

Turner moved his arm and hand to Alex's shoulder and, like a parent guiding a young child to sit down, he gleefully replied, "Dante! I have heard so much about you. Come into my office, sit, please."

"I hope what you have heard about me has been mostly pleasurable?" Alex jokingly responded.

"Oh, absolutely! All good. I have been Glen Firestone's friend for many years. When he called to add you to the Johnson Trust, I had no doubt you were a stellar citizen," Jim answered in a way to repress any discomfort Alex might be feeling at meeting him.

"How do you know Glen?" Alex innocently questioned.

Turner answered very quickly. "Pastor Firestone has been my pastor for several years. My wife and I helped the Firestone's start Seaside Community Church. We were with them from the start. My wife's family had a farm here in La Grande and when her mom and dad passed, we decided to come here and try farming. As you can see, I still do some lawyering to pay the bills."

Alex chuckled at Jim's statement and nodded in affirmation that he knew exactly what he was talking about.

"So, I assume your visit today isn't just to meet me?" Turner said, tongue in cheek.

"No, not that meeting you hasn't been a pleasure, but I wanted to stop and let you know this office will be receiving an invoice from La Grande Appliance. They're delivering a refrigerator freezer to the Johnson property. I just wanted to see if you needed my signature to release the funds from the Trust."

"No problemo, son. I don't need a signature. Now that I've met you, if you need anything, just call me. Here's my card with my personal cell phone number," Turner responded with all sense of sincerity.

Alex stood up and extended his hand towards Jim Turner. "Thanks so much, Mr. Turner." As Alex began his departure from the meeting with Jim Turner the lawyer stopped him with a question.

"If you don't mind me asking, the Johnson property has been abandoned for several years now. In fact, you might say there are several greedy property owners around here that would like the mayor to exercise imminent domain based on the condition of the house. Truth is, they know they can manipulate the mayor into dividing the Johnson property up so they can get their hands on that rich farmland."

Alex turned to look at Jim Turner. "The Trust has a tenant staying out there. He doesn't require much attention, but his icebox is broken."

"Hmm, a tenant, huh? That's gonna make it a sticky wicket for the mayor and his minions. Makes my job easier," Turner chuckled under his breath.

Alex walked towards the front door and gave one last wave back to Jim Turner and said, "That is why we have you, Jim. We know you'll keep the wrong noses out of our business."

Jim pondered Alex's last statement. It was a response that brought with it an air of mystery. He shrugged it off and turned to go back to his office. Just as he reached the door, he was startled to hear an ambulance, with its sirens screaming, pass by his front window. "Hope whoever's in there isn't hurt bad," Turner whispered to himself as it sped away from his office towards the local hospital.

Chapter 29: Exposed

GARY HARDING DROVE AS FAST AS HE COULD to keep up with the ambulance. He couldn't shake what he had just seen from his mind. The voice that was coming from Shannon was not hers. "If it wasn't hers, then who, or what, was it?" Gary wondered. As the ambulance reached the entrance to the La Grande Memorial Hospital, Gary searched frantically for an open parking spot. He was tempted to just pull up behind the ambulance so he could see how Shannon was doing. "After all, I am the mayor. They can't tell me not to park there!" Gary thought to himself. Luckily, he found a parking spot near the entrance, threw his truck into park and exited as fast as he could to run to the ambulance.

The EMT's pulled the gurney that contained Shannon from the back of the ambulance. Gary was worried to see all the medical apparatus attached to her. He ran to her side as they wheeled her into the emergency room. He felt better to see that she was awake and seemed more alert than when he last saw her. Once inside the emergency room, medical staff scurried about her like ants on a mission to find food.

A nurse came over to Gary and began to question him about what had occurred at the farm. He answered to the best of his recollection but didn't tell the nurse about the strange voice and words that had come from Shannon. After drilling Gary for as much information as she could gather, the nurse released Gary to come to Shannon's side. He held her hand up to his lips. Shannon stared blankly at the gesture, but her eyes did contact Gary's to let him know she recognized him.

"My dear Shannon. I am so worried about you. I will have these doctors and nurses do whatever it takes to make you better. I love you, Shannon Brown," Gary made no effort to disguise his actions or feelings to the medical staff that was attending to Shannon. Nor did he seem to be conscious of anybody else who might be standing in close enough proximity to see and hear his tribute to his mistress. In fact, just outside the room where Shannon was receiving care from the medical staff, and her boss was singing his love for her, stood Aspen Harding, with a stream of tears running down her cheeks.

Chapter 3o:
A Demons Plan

After leaving their home state of Oregon, the Dantes arrived for the first stop in their trek to Colorado in Boise, Idaho. Pulling into the motel, Alex located a spot for the U-haul near the back and met Courtney near the entrance. Courtney produced a much-needed stretch as she went to get Annie out of her car seat. "That was a long day. I needed to get Annie and me out of that car!" Courtney explained to Alex, although it was preaching to the choir.

Alex answered while bending over to touch his toes in his version of stretching his muscles, "Did Annabel do okay? She seems to be in a good mood."

"She did much better than I expected. I was a little worried we bit off too much to chew on our first leg to Colorado," Courtney acknowledged.

The trio made their way to their motel room after checking in. Looking around the room, both Courtney and Alex were pleased at how clean and comfy it appeared. Courtney had arranged for a crib to be delivered to the room and Alex checked it out to make sure it was steady and safe. "It looks fine," he acknowledged.

Too tired to go out for dinner, the Dante's ordered pizza to be delivered to the room. Both ate the pizza in a hurried manner in anticipation of getting to bed as quick as they could. Courtney changed Annie's diaper and dressed her in soft cotton jammies. Alex laid down on the bed and fluffed the white down feather pillow. He watched as Courtney fed Annabel. Alex treasured those moments of bonding between mother and daughter. Although he never asked his own mother if she breastfed, it didn't really matter. His bond with his mother was special.

Alex watched as Courtney placed an already sleeping Annabel in the crib. Climbing in to bed next to her husband, she sought the comfort of his arm to cradle around her. Within minutes, Courtney was fast asleep. Alex gently slid the arm that was holding Courtney from under her and reached over to turn off the light. Just as soon as he found the perfect position for his head in the pillow, exhaustion overtook Alex, and he fell asleep.

Sometime in his slumber, Alex began to dream. In his dream he was sitting in the meager side chair that adorned the hotel room. Next to him, in a matching chair, was Courtney. It was a vivid dream. He could see the contours of her face and the small dark mole on her neck. Alex had never had as vivid a dream as this.

Suddenly, standing before them was their old ghostly friend, Annabel Perkins. Alex watched as Annabel went to the crib to capture a look at the small child sleeping there. "She is truly beautiful. Such a gift from God," Annabel Perkins spoke without removing her gaze from the child.

"Yes, she is, dear Annabel," Courtney replied.

The spirit of Annabel turned her attention towards Alex and Courtney and instead of her usual smile, her face seemed sullen and concerned. "I have come to you in your dreams. Both of you are seeing and conversing with me in your dreams. I want you to know this, that each of you are having the same dream. What I am here to tell you is extremely important and you both must follow my instructions very carefully. Especially you, Alex. I say this to you as a commandment from our Lord and Savior."

Alex looked over at Courtney, who now had as equally a concerned look on her face as their ghostly friend.

Annabel yielded to a vision of movement that was behind her and heading towards the crib of the infant Annabel. Alex could not discern who or what was moving towards his daughter's crib, but it deeply disturbed him. Annabel Perkins pointed towards the apparition that had invaded their space. With his defensive mechanisms on high alert, Alex began to make the form into something he recognized. The glimpses of ginger colored hair on the specter's head and face brought Alex to the realization that he had seen this figure before. Alex knew at this moment; a demon had entered their room and his dream.

Annabel Perkins, for the first time since she had joined in the spiritual communion with Alex and Courtney, suddenly became stern with Alex. She returned her focus to Alex and held out the palm of her single hand with ghostly fingers upright in defiance. "Do not intervene, Alex. Little Annabel is not in danger. This is the demon, Orin. He is most vile and deviant. He was sent by Lucifer to get to you. Lucifer must learn the extent of your powers. His very existence depends on it. Orin has devised a plan to discover that knowledge and deliver it to his master! And with that knowledge, this demon will expose the sanctuary of the object of Lucifer's obsession, which is to discover the location of the demon, Gayland."

"Gayland? Why would Lucifer care about finding Gayland?" Alex quizzed the spirit of Annabel Perkins.

"Because, dear Alex, with the power of his nemesis, the God of the Universe dwelling within you, you chastised his dominion. It really isn't Gayland, it's you that irritates him."

Alex, with a perplexed look on his face, turned his head once again to look at Courtney. Her look of concern had turned to horror. "What is the plan of this demon, Orin? What is he planning to do to get to my husband and learn the extent of his abilities? And how will that expose Gayland's location?" Courtney pleaded with Annabel to divulge this mystery of Orin's plot.

"Orin will attempt to indwell the precious child, Annabel!"

Courtney gasped and Alex jumped to his feet.

"I will vanquish him! He will be sorry he ever conjured this idea!" Alex pounded his chest in a defiant manner.

Annabel Perkins stood before Alex Dante. He instantly felt her calm engulf him. It was like nothing he had ever felt before. He was certain her spirit had passed through him, and he sat back down in his chair.

The spirit Annabel returned to address Alex and Courtney. With Alex still under the influence of Annabel's calming, she spoke softly, "Alex, you shall not intervene. This has been commanded of you." She turned towards Courtney and provided her comfort. "The child is not in danger. This I have told you. The demon Orin's plan was to indwell young Annabel and wait until she grew in age and knowledge. Orin's gamble is the belief that the child will come to have the same abilities as her father. She will come to know just how Alex moves as the Host of Gabriel. This knowledge will then be Orin's to deliver to his master."

"But what are we to do when this happens? When will this happen? I am so afraid for little Annie!" Courtney cried in a frantic manner.

A smile once again returned to Annabel Perkins' ghostly face and she spoke calmly to Alex and Courtney, "You needn't do anything. Do you not know that children receive the protection of Jesus? Innocence has no knowledge of good or evil. The holy spirit protects the innocent hearts of the children until the day they can come to God on their own."

Alex sighed as his shoulders relaxed from Annabel's words. "Yes, I knew this. Children are protected until the day of accountability."

"Bless you, dear Alex. Now you know why you should not fear for little Annie. Orin has no knowledge of this protection. His master certainly does not, or chooses not to tell him," Annabel Perkins explained.

"When will Orin attempt to indwell my baby?" Courtney asked with great anxiety.

"It has happened while you both slept. Alex saw the demon in this dream. What he saw was truly happening," Annabel revealed to her mortal friends.

"What happens now to Orin? Is he returned down the portal to face his master's wrath? If so, good. Pain and torture in Hell are too good for him," Alex let his anger and emotions take the best of him.

Annabel Perkins seemed to forgive, and more so, understand Alex's statement. "No, dear Alex. God has dispatched one of his most mighty Angels to deal with Orin. It is up to our Lord to determine Orin's fate."

Alex quizzed his spirit host, "Has Gabriel come to protect me and my family?"

Annabel laughed a ghostly laugh that echoed like they were in a limestone canyon. Once she regained her composure, she answered Alex. "Gabriel is mighty and powerful. This you well know. We are in a spiritual battle. It is only going to be worse one day. This time God has sent a warrior. A mighty warrior. The Archangel, Michael."

Chapter 31:
Evil Makes His Move

ORIN MANIFESTED HIS MORTAL APPEARANCE as he crept towards the crib that held the infant Dante child. He calculated that his mortal persona might not alert the sleeping Alex Dante to his presence. His demon mind also calculated that the child might not be as alarmed by his unassuming physical presence thereby alerting and waking the sleeping Dante's. As Orin came near to the infant, he was pleased to see it was comfortably in its mortal sleep. This will make his indwelling much easier.

There came a moment that he was startled by the restlessness of both Dante and his mate. It appears they were both disturbed in their slumber. This was curious to Orin as he had seen mortals sleep in what seemed like peace. He had never known sleep, or peace. He decided that this restlessness that Dante showed revealed he was tormented by Gabriel's God.

"Hmm, serves you right. You made a poor choice on who to follow, Dante," These sarcastic thoughts passed through the demon's mind.

Having grown tired of tracking and following the Dante's, Orin decided it was time to inhabit the infant. He had grown impatient and decided that it would give him time to discover just what it was like to indwell a mortal child. After all, he had never done this before. All his previous souls were delivered as adult mortals. Orin tried not to display his eagerness. His impatience was partially due to his curiosity.

In the confines of this dark room, in the realm of Boise, Idaho, Orin would become one with the offspring of Dante. He came to the edge of the wood structure that confined the child. Orin took a moment to gaze upon the mortal. It seemed so innocent. He really wasn't sure how he would manifest evil into this mortal's actions. His plan had no reference to call upon. This indwelling would need to be learned as he went.

Just before returning to his demon spirit state to begin the indwelling, Orin heard the audible voice of Alex Dante call out, "Stop!" This sudden reverberation of Alex Dante's voice startled Orin. He stood silent in his mortal state of a short, scruffy, ginger man, reluctant to move. This paralysis was foreign to Orin. Why should he be afraid of this mere mortal human? He could easily enter this man's child and it would be too late for him to do anything about it.

Alex Dante returned to restless sleep and Orin heard no more cries come from the sleeping man. Orin felt another foreign feeling which was relief. The demon transfigured into his spirit and hovered above the infant child of Alex Dante. A whirlwind of evil overcame his demon intellect.

With many centuries of past existence far from love, the companionship and calm of a world Orin had once known invaded his very thoughts and he repelled them. If he had the ability to indwell a human in his mortal persona, his eyes would be rolled up into the back of his head with sweat pouring from his mortal brow.

Orin, now prepared, began the indwell. The unknown was before him, and he felt excitement at what this experience would bring. Like a man who was out of breath after exerting himself, Orin took a demon breath of repulsive evil and perused the environment of the child's mind. Except there was nothingness.

"Have I failed to indwell and inhabit the child?" Orin questioned. Not requiring the assistance of mortal light to see his surroundings, Orin quickly refocused his demon eyes expecting to see the room where he had just recently dwelled. There was no infant child. No restless sleeping Alex Dante and his mate. He was in the dark, gray cave of his retreat where he had plotted and planned his attack on Alex Dante, using the child to perpetrate his evil for the benefit of his master.

Orin was stunned and confused. How was it he was now here? This place that is his sanctuary of choice. Damp, stark and void of any happiness. Suddenly his demon eyes were blinded by the reflection of light. Light that emitted every essence that Orin feared, and he covered his eyes to avoid the meaning and source of the light. Soon, Orin could begin to focus on the magnificence before him and it was not his master, Lucifer. The light belonged to something he feared far more.

Eventually, Orin could make out the entire figure of a warrior Angel. Michael, the Archangel, adorned in the full armor of God, and in his right hand he wielded the sword of the Spirit, which was the manifestation of the Word of God. For the only time in his centuries of demonic existence, every molecule of Orin knew true terror.

Chapter 32:
Moment of Panic

Sitting in his rocking chair, Gayland understood what he had just seen at the entrance of the gate to his farm. The mortals that had come to invade his sanctuary, without invitation, were thwarted by Alex Dante's protection. "What a mighty mortal he is. My former master has no idea just how powerful this mortal is," Gayland mused as he sipped his iced tea.

A demon had reared himself from the convulsing body of the mortal female that was lying in the dirt before the gate. Gayland was not sure if the demon had witnessed him on the opposite side of the gate. That demon appeared to be in torment. Gayland considered, for a moment, that the demon might have recognized him and could return to his master to relay that information. "I have seen the end. It does not turn out well for you, Lucifer. If coming to my sanctuary is something you desire, then bring it on," Gayland thought to himself with all the confidence of the ages.

Gary Harding received encouragement from the nurses that were attending to Shannon Brown that she was resting comfortably, and that it might be a good time for him to go home and get some rest. He reluctantly agreed, and as he stood up from Shannon's bedside, he leaned over and kissed her cheek. The demon that indwelled her was repulsed. He was always repulsed by actions of affection towards his host, but he tolerated this mortal attention because it was a means to achieve his plan. A plan that would lead to power and that power would yield evil.

As Gary walked away from the entrance of the hospital, towards his truck, he stopped and looked back at the hospital with a forlorn expression on his face. As tired as he was, the puzzled thoughts about the voice he heard coming from his beloved Shannon invaded every fiber of his being. Without looking towards his truck, Gary pressed the button to unlock the door. Climbing into the cab, he started the engine and placed the truck into drive. He wouldn't rest until he could make some sense out of what had happened that day. As day yielded to dusk, Gary Harding pulled the truck out onto Main Street heading in the direction of Johnson's farm, and hopefully to finding some answers that made sense.

Gayland enjoyed dusk. With night just around the corner, it brought with it not only dark, but for a demon like himself, peace. The cat sat beside his chair on the porch. The feline also enjoyed night. It was the time for hunting and its evening meal.

Gayland glanced at his jar of iced tea and noticed the ice that once accompanied the brown liquid had melted. "Time for more ice," Gayland spoke as he pushed away from his rocking chair and proceeded to the kitchen to the mortal appliance that made the delightful cubes of frozen water he now worshipped.

Reaching the refrigerator, Gayland flung open the upper section where the ice cubes are formed. A puzzled and somewhat panicked look possessed Gayland's expression. Dipping his demon finger into the metal tray where the cubes were formed from water, he felt no cold.

Nothing solid. All he could feel was the wetness of the water he had poured into the tray a long time ago.

Gayland, for the first time since he could recall, felt helpless. His demon hands grasped his head, and he glanced back and forth looking for help, but none was available.

Just then, out of the corner of his demon eye, Gayland could see the glowing orbs of a mortal carriage stopping outside of the gate entrance to his sanctuary. "Not now!" Gayland cried out in frustration of being interrupted at such a time as this. He slammed the door to the freezer and moved with supernatural speed to his side of the gate.

Immediately he recognized the mortal carriage as the same one that had come earlier. Yet, this time, the tall mortal that appeared earlier was alone. The demon that had accompanied him earlier was not there. Gayland stood at the gate observing the man as he moved from the vehicle and stood quietly outside the gate.

Gary Harding turned on the large flashlight he carried from his truck and shined the light towards the steps that led to the porch of the decaying Johnson farmhouse. The light caressed each object it enveloped until it fell upon a large jar with a brown liquid resting on the top step of the stairs leading up to the porch. "I'll be damned! It's there, just like Hastings said," Gary spoke out loud although there was nobody there to listen.

Setting the flashlight down, Gary used the headlights of his truck to illuminate the chain that held the gate to the post. As he began to unravel the chain to gain entrance to the farm, he saw two small headlights from another vehicle off in the distance which seemed to be heading his way. With each passing moment the lights grew larger and brighter. "Who in the tarnation could that be?" Gary thought to himself.

Gayland was not pleased. His demon existence depended on the frozen cubes of water that, prior to this moment, were always available. This distraction was not welcome. This mortal intrusion defiled his sanctuary.

As a black and white sedan pulled up next to his truck, Gary immediately recognized the decal on the side of the car, La Grande County Sheriff. Stepping from the car, a large pot-bellied man placed his cowboy hat on his head and strode towards Gary. "Evening, Mayor. Thought I might find you here," The overweight man nonchalantly called out towards Gary like two men who just happened to come across each other at a local ballgame.

"Sheriff, I'm surprised to see you here," Gary responded to the arrival of his recent companion.

Sheriff Parker had been in his law enforcement position in La Grande for over forty years. The lack of crime in La Grande and the availability of good donuts and pastries had obviously contributed to Parker's physique. Sheriff Parker walked to Gary Harding's side and gently pulled his hand from the chain that held the gate shut. "Jim Turner came by my office today. He said that you and the Co-Op had been snooping into having the city claim the rights to Johnson's farm. Something like, imminent domain due to structural safety, or something along those lines," Parker explained.

"We're looking into it, Sheriff. It's my responsibility as mayor to make things safe for my constituents." Harding replied with a politician's banter.

"Well, that's why I'm here, Mayor. You got no reason now to trespass."

"Trespass? Just look at this place. It's about ready to fall down!" Gary excitedly answered. Shining his flashlight up towards the porch and, with the beam of light landing on the jar, Gary pointed and called out, "Look, we even have a squatter problem. Just look at that jar of tea on the porch!"

"Exactly," Parker announced in total affirmation of what Harding had just pointed out.

"What do you mean by 'exactly'", Sheriff?"

"The Trust has hired a caretaker for the farmhouse. He's living here now, so I need you to get in your truck and go home," Parker revealed.

"Caretaker? Who in the hell is this caretaker?" Gary questioned as a child who had been caught with his hand in the cookie jar.

"I'm not sure, Gary. I haven't met him. The Trust says his name is Gayland Johnson. Apparently, he's a distant relative of old man Johnson. They vetted him, so that's good enough for me."

A short time later a dejected Gary Harding and Sheriff Parker climbed back into their respective vehicles and drove back down the dirt, wash boarded road, and away from Johnson's farm.

Gayland stood where he had always been as he watched the conversation unfold between the two men. With a smug look on his demon face he smiled. "Gayland Johnson. I like that." But with the ending of the momentary pleasure of the events that had just unfolded, reality crept back into Gayland's thoughts. Was he to live out the rest of his peaceful existence without ice? He longed for the cool sensation and peaceful relief the frozen water cubes brought to his existence.

For a moment, peace on Johnson's farm was nowhere to be found. And just who in the hell was Gayland Johnson, caretaker? That was a truthful question as he didn't even have the power to do anything about the lack of ice at Johnson farm.

Chapter 33:
Awakening

ALEX LEAPED FROM HIS HOTEL BED, almost simultaneously with Courtney. Both scurried to Annabel's crib, meeting there at the same time. Courtney scooped up her child, holding her close. Alex placed one hand on Courtney's neck and at the same time wrapped his arm around them as if to protect both from an unknown assassin.

Little Annie, with eyes open and beaming alertly at the antics of her parents, smiled. Courtney and Alex breathed for the first time since their sojourn to Annabel's crib. "She's fine, Court. She's fine," Alex said as he labored to gain oxygen back into his lungs.

Courtney, straining to hold back the tears that were streaming down her cheeks, looked up at her husband with inquiring eyes and asked, "Did Annabel Perkins visit you in your dream?"

"She did. Annabel was here for both of us. Our Lord sent her to us as a messenger. What we dreamt was really happening."

"Then our poor little Annie really was in danger?" Courtney anxiously asked.

Alex released Courtney and the baby and sat down on the bed. Heavy into contemplation and trying to understand everything that had happened, Alex looked up at Courtney and answered earnestly, "Court, you, Annie, and mostly me, are all targets of the evil one. We know that, especially now. The demon that sought to indwell our baby was doing so to get to me. He's been tracking us since we were at the park in Hillsborough. I saw him there and I've seen him since."

"Alex, please tell me he's gone forever."

"Yes, my love, that demon will never try and hurt our family again. He's gone. No child can be indwelled. They're protected by our Lord and Savior. Our gracious God sent the Angel warrior, Michael, to deal with that vile creature. I'm thankful for that," Alex answered with the grace that had been bestowed on him by God.

A curious expression was etched on Courtney's face as she asked Alex, "What becomes of the demon?"

"I'm not exactly sure. I do know one thing though," Alex replied.

"What is that?" Courtney inquired.

"I'm glad I'm not Orin."

The Dante's took the rest of the morning to recover from their ordeal. They held and played with little Annie. They cherished each other. They prayed together before packing up their belongings and heading down the highway towards their new lives in Colorado. Alex wished they could be in one vehicle. Having his family closer would have brought him comfort.

As they made their way across the southern border of Idaho, Alex was astonished at the difference in terrain from his home state of Oregon. Idaho was farm country. Flat and fertile, but definitely flat. As the convoy traveled through Utah and into Wyoming, none of their nightly stops provided any dreams of Annabel Perkins.

Having a heavenly messenger was a blessing from God, but deep down, Alex and Courtney were relieved that no more revelations of demons stalking them had happened, even though Alex was constantly on alert for their presence.

The trek across Wyoming was as flat and frankly boring as Idaho to Alex. He began to become a little skeptical of just what they were getting themselves into by moving to Colorado. If the landscape was like what he was seeing in southern Wyoming, it would take some getting used to, being from the Great Northwest.

They spent their final road night in Cheyenne, Wyoming, before making the turn south, down Interstate 25. Just after the turnoff for Ft. Collins, Colorado, Alex began to feel some relief. Off to his right, towards the west, he began to see evidence of the Rocky Mountains.

"This is looking up," he said to himself as he dialed Courtney's cellphone. After one quick ring, Courtney answered the call. She was crying.

"What's wrong? Courtney, what's the matter?" Alex quizzed her with much anxiety.

"Nothing is wrong. I'm just happy to see mountains," Courtney Dante blurted out.

Chapter 34: Battle

ORIN HISSED LIKE A SNAKE AT MICHAEL. The arena to which he had been brought, after the failure of his plan to indwell the young Dante child, was strategically not to his liking. It was desperate enough that he would have to battle here, but to battle the likes of Michael made things much worse.

Orin couldn't help but marvel at the Angel in front of him. Michael was everything that he, Orin, was not. The arena was devoid of any light except the grays and sepia hues that encompassed it, but Michael was magnificent. His armor shone with the brightness of solid gold, forged into plates adorned with scribe and design. His light was as bright as the sun and it blinded Orin.

"Hissing is how you greet me, demon?" Michael requested an answer from the cowering demon.

"I have no words for you, Angel. My master will be here soon, and he can discuss with you the poor decision you have made to interfere with me."

Michael, whose physical face could not be discerned by Orin because of the light emitting from around him, spoke, "Orin, it was not myself that interfered. You and your master decided to tempt the true God of the Universe.

A mortal infant is not available to your kind. They are precious to God, and he alone protects them."

Orin spewed morsels of vile from his mouth, "Then why are you here? I am of the Legion of Lucifer; I am precious to him!"

"Your master does not come. He exists on borrowed time. You are just one of many pawns at his service. He knows better than to challenge me for the likes of you," Michael professed.

Orin began to size up his foe, knowing that he was most likely on his own and out of his league. "Then tell me, Angel, if protection of the Dante child was so important as to send the Mighty Archangel, Michael, why didn't Dante just do it himself? Are his powers so weak that your God must send you?"

"Vile demon, Alex Dante is a mortal man. Until the second coming of our Lord, mortals must abide by the Word of God. Soon, Alex Dante will be the gatekeeper for your master, and your kind. But until that time, just as you cannot kill a human by your hands, so be it for the human!" Michael answered with the power of a hundred earthquakes.

"And what of you, Michael? Are we to battle to see who vanquishes who?"

Michael brandished his gleaming sword and pointed it towards Orin. "There will be no battle today, demon. Know that the mortal Alex Dante has the power to bind you and your master. Ye shall know that Jesus is Lord."

A confused Orin pondered the words that Michael had just spoken. "So, what are we to do now, Mighty Angel? Are we to sit and have mortal tea and talk about how glorious we both are?"

Suddenly, the light surrounding the Archangel Michael was gone. Orin looked around to see if Michael and his sword were poised to attack. Nothing. Only the stark, damp nothingness of the arena existed before him.

What a dismal depressing place this was. Devoid of any reasonable existence for Angel or demon.

Searching his demon intellect for any opening leading away from this arena, Orin began to panic and with desperation called out for his Legion to come to him. None under his command came. He called for his master, Lucifer. After a few demon moments, Orin began to understand the words that Michael had proclaimed. This arena wasn't the place to bring him glory. Either in victory over the Archangel Michael, or even defeat at the sword of Michael. This place was like he didn't exist. Not to his master, Alex Dante, or his Legion.

This gray tomb was his prison, and he was bound, and soon, torment would invade his demon mind with no relief to remove it.

Chapter 35:
Deceit Lays Its Future

HE SAT IN THE DRIVEWAY of his modest La Grande home. It was a three-bedroom, two-bathroom ranch house. The home was really nothing to boast about, but it was his and Aspen's first home. He had grand plans for his future and this home was just the beginning. He dreamed of someday living in Salem, Oregon. Two children, one boy and one girl, and he was the Governor of Oregon. Until that dream could come true, Aspen always did her best to make this house a home, but it was his dream, not necessarily hers. That dream died for Aspen but was revived once again for Gary when Shannon Brown came into his life.

Gary sat in the running truck, reluctant to turn off the engine and retreat to his house. He was certain that Aspen would be standing there, wanting answers to where he had been. He really didn't want to confront her. All he wanted was to be by Shannon's side.

As he walked up the pathway that led to his front door, Gary noticed that the house looked unusually dark. The front porch light was not lit as it normally was when Gary would be arriving home after dark. He grabbed the doorknob to open the door, but it was locked. Gary pulled out his house key and inserted it into the lock. Proceeding into the front entry of his home, the entire house was dark.

He was confused by all of this. It appeared Aspen wasn't home. She never ventured outside the house without him. "How weird," Gary thought to himself. Fumbling for a switch on the lamp near the front door, Gary illuminated the living room. He was alone. He threw his keys on the side table that held the lamp and proceeded to the kitchen. There, in the kitchen, in the cabinet above the sink, was a bottle of whiskey that he desperately needed right now.

Gary grabbed a small glass from another cabinet and, opening the bottle, poured the whiskey into the glass until it almost overflowed. He brought the glass to his lips and in one complete action, drank the contents of the glass. As he was putting the glass down on the kitchen counter to pour himself another drink, he spotted an envelope sitting next to the coffee maker. Gary picked up the envelope and saw his name written on the front. He recognized Aspen's handwriting.

Nervously opening the envelope to remove the letter contained inside, Gary read the note:

Gary,
I now know for sure what I have been suspecting for quite a while. You were not aware that I had come to the hospital when I heard there had been an accident or something at Johnson's farm.

I was worried that something had happened to you. Yes, worried that the person I loved had been injured or perhaps worse. You read that last sentence correctly. I used the word loved.

What I saw and heard at the hospital taught me that I have been a fool. Maybe not in the beginning, but a fool now. I am leaving you, Gary.

You have made your choice. It wasn't my choice, but yours! What I witnessed at the hospital told me that you no longer love me and probably haven't for quite a while.

Don't try and contact me. I will not answer your call. I hope Shannon isn't as naïve to your hurtful ways as I was.

Aspen

Gary put the letter down on the counter. In a way, he was relieved the truth had been exposed. He poured himself another glass of whiskey and carried it into the living room. He sat down in the recliner that was his usual chair of choice and drank the glass of whiskey. Soon after finishing his drink, Gary Harding fell asleep, not thinking about how he had hurt his wife but wondering what his future with Shannon Brown could be.

Chapter 36:
The Risk

THE DEMON THAT INDWELLED SHANNON BROWN hovered about her hospital room impatiently. He had never experienced what had happened to him earlier at the gate. In his being bound, and the pain and torment that followed, he needed to understand. His confusion led to the realization that the only one that could answer his questions would be his master.

His demon mind searched for just what to do next. He couldn't fathom leaving his host to travel down the portal to try and gain audience with Lucifer. Leaving a host was forbidden by his master. Doing so could lead to an eternal death. Still, in the struggle with being forbidden to enter the gate with his human host, he was sure he saw another demon on the other side. "Why was that demon allowed to remain inside the gate?" He pondered with the need to find resolution.

The demon decided the despair he was suffering justified the risk of leaving the woman. It was a risk he must take. As the demon left his host, he watched her, as she seemed to be in distress. Thrashing back and forth in her hospital bed was causing alarms to go off, alerting the nursing staff to come running to her bedside. Just as quickly as her convulsing had started, it ended, and Shannon Brown was found in a fetal position laying on the floor.

Satisfied that his former host had not succumbed to death upon his leaving, as that would have created a real problem, the demon exited the physical location of the hospital in La Grande and supernaturally headed toward the portal that would lead him down the abyssal, and directly to his master, Lucifer. It would have been quite uncomfortable explaining to his master that her soul was now ready to deliver, but unfortunately, she was no longer indwelled.

Chapter 37:
The Delivery

THE DIRECTIONS THAT ALEX HAD PROVIDED for Tyler and Cindy to help find Gayland's farm proved to be easy to follow. They traveled a short distance down a washboard dirt road until they pulled up outside a rusting metal gate that would lead to a dilapidated old farmhouse less than 200 yards ahead of them. A metal sign had been recently hung on the gate. Tyler could tell the sign was new because it showed no rust or decay. It read "NO TRESPASSING".

After removing the chain that held the gate from swinging freely, Tyler climbed back in the SUV and glanced at Cindy who was staring directly ahead at the driveway that led to the old farmhouse.

"Are you okay, Cinderoo? Is this too much for you to handle?" Tyler quizzed her.

"No, I'm fine. Just a little nervous knowing a demon lives here." Cindy answered without removing her gaze from the farmhouse.

The couple drove past the gate and brought their SUV to a stop near the steps that led up to the porch of the farmhouse. "Do you see something?" Tyler inquired, based on his wife having not diverted her eyes away from the screen door that led inside the house.

"No. I just have a sense that he's here. Somewhere close. Watching us."

This statement by Cindy caused the hair on the back of Tyler's neck to stand up. He determined he must take the lead and started moving to the first step to make the climb up the stairs. When he was about to place his right foot on the step, Tyler was startled by a stray cat that had appeared and was rubbing against his right leg and worn cowhide boot.

Tyler chuckled, after his heart began to beat normally, and called out to Cindy, who remained stationary at the passenger side of the SUV, "Hey, Cindy, I think I just found the caretaker!"

At last Cindy broke her stare away from the front of the farmhouse and answered her husband. "Well, he must like sun tea," as she pointed towards the jar sitting on the top porch step.

"Alex did say the tea would be here. He didn't say anything about a cat, but he did call out the tea all right."

Cindy slowly walked over to where Tyler had begun his journey up the stairs and took his hand in her right hand. She wasn't about to attempt the climb without him. With her left hand she bent down to stroke the head and ears of the cat. "It's purring. I guess it isn't afraid of demons," Cindy revealed in an almost sarcastic tone.

They walked up the steps and both stared intently at the jar of tea as they passed by it. The porch creaked with each step they took towards the screen door that would allow them access to the home. Their eyes glanced to their left, and they noticed two wooden rocking chairs sitting parallel to each other allowing a perfect view of the acreage of the old barley farm, but most importantly, the gate that allowed access to the farm.

"Interesting. There isn't a mason jar sitting on the old table next to the chair. Alex said it would most likely be there." Tyler mentioned with the tone of someone building a jigsaw puzzle.

"Yes, interesting," Cindy answered, but she was clearly not focused on the fact.

Tyler opened the screen door, and it screeched like a banshee flying above on a haunted night. Cindy followed him in, not about to let go of his hand. The couple stood side by side as they perused the contents of the interior of the old farmhouse. Dust on almost every piece of furniture and the surrounding trinkets would indicate that no human had lived here for quite some time.

Cindy pointed towards the kitchen counter. Next to an old rusty farmhouse sink and a very antiquated Frigidaire refrigerator sat a mason jar, with tea filled almost to the top. Tyler walked over to the jar and picked it up. He held the jar up to his nose and took a deep breath. "It smells fresh, Cindy. This tea was recently poured."

Cindy turned towards the living room, which was open to the kitchen, and spoke loud enough for Angels and demons to hear from miles off. "I am Cindy McIntyre. This is my husband, Tyler. We are invited here by our brother in Christ, Alex Dante. We mean you no harm, Gayland. We know you are here and can hear me. We cannot see you. God hasn't anointed us with that gift, but we have been asked by Alex to attend to you, as you are in need. I cannot see you, but I sense you. Do not fear our presence. My senses do not deceive me. They are always on high alert since I was redeemed from the clutches of a demon you know as Demetri."

A tap came from outside on the screen door that sent Cindy and Tyler almost through the roof. Tyler regained his composure and went to discover a young man with a clipboard standing outside on the porch. "Sorry I interrupted you folks. I'm Paul, from La Grande Appliances. I have a refrigerator delivery for you."

With all the intensity of the mason jar discovery, and with Cindy speaking directly to Gayland, both Tyler and Cindy had failed to notice a white paneled delivery truck pull up at the farmhouse. Tyler bent over slightly and placed both hands on his knees and began to laugh. "Yes, yes…we were expecting you. Come in, come on in, Paul."

The young man affirmed he was in the right place and waved at Tyler through the screen door. He entered and spoke, "I guess you want the new refrigerator in the same place as the old one?"

Still startled, Tyler replied, "Yes, yes, that will be fine."

Paul walked over to the old Frigidaire and confirmed with Cindy and Tyler, "Yep, the compressor's shot. I'm surprised this old fridge lasted for as long as it did. I'm gonna fetch my dolly and I'll pull this old one out. It's on the order to take this one with me for disposal."

Tyler smiled and confirmed that was correct. With Paul having left to get the appliance dolly from his truck, Cindy came over to Tyler to be embraced in his arms. "I'll be glad when this is done. I think this demon business is for the birds!" Cindy said with half humor and half sincerity.

Paul returned to the kitchen with the dolly that would remove the old refrigerator. He placed the strap around the old refrigerator and tilted the appliance back to begin to roll it out to his delivery truck waiting outside. "Do you need any help?" Tyler offered to Paul, who was now holding the full weight of the old refrigerator.

"Naw, I got this. Maybe hold the screen door open for me," Paul replied, showing he had a lot of experience moving appliances. As Paul gently maneuvered the old refrigerator through the door and out onto the porch, Gayland was experiencing something rare. High anxiety. He was witnessing what he determined was a breach of the commitment that Alex had made to him. His ice was going away and somehow his peace would be diminished.

Shortly after Gayland saw his reason for giving up his demon responsibilities and living alone at this, his sanctuary, being hauled away, he heard a noise out on his porch. The human that had carried away his tranquility had returned. Not empty handed, but with something like what he had removed.

Tyler held the door open for Paul as he rolled in a brand-new refrigerator. He lowered it down in the same place as the old refrigerator, removed the straps from around it and pushed it into position. Cindy admired the new refrigerator.

She brushed her fingers across the surface and opened the doors that concealed the freezer section and food storage. "So nice, it's a side by side. What a nice gift for a dem…," Cindy stopped in mid-sentence before blurting out the obvious words that would have made the appliance delivery person look at her with confusion and begin questioning her sanity. "A nice gift to demonstrate just how great this renovation will be," She quickly summoned the words to save the exposure of the real reason they were there.

"Yep, it's a beaut. I was wondering on the way out here, why not have an automatic ice maker, but now I see this old house doesn't have a water line to support it. Ya know, they're easy to install and running a line should be easy," Paul offered as he plugged in the new refrigerator. As he wrapped the strap around the dolly, Paul handed some paperwork to Tyler to sign.

He thanked the McIntyre's for shopping at La Grande Appliance and rolled the dolly out the front screen door and down the porch steps towards his delivery truck. As he climbed into the cab, Paul saw Tyler frantically come waving and running out the front door and with one leap, hurtle down the porch steps. "Thank God, I caught you before you left! I need the metal ice trays out of the old refrigerator!"

Perplexed by Tyler's request, Paul exited the cab of the delivery truck and swung up and opened the door to the back of the truck. Handing the old metal trays to Tyler, Paul shrugged and said, "Hey, to each their own."

As Tyler waved goodbye to Paul and watched the truck disappear down the old dirt road, he went back into the farmhouse holding the metal trays like a newborn baby.

Chapter 38:
Lucifer's Discovery

LUCIFER WAS IMPATIENT. He paced around his cathedral of despair as a mortal who was waiting on a delivery of an important package. Having received no reports on the indwelling of the Dante child, he began to question why he had agreed to Orin's plan to use this possession to learn the location of Gayland's sanctuary. His being obsessed with both finding Gayland and the challenge of discovering Alex Dante's abilities shouldn't be distracting him like this. He had much more important things to do.

"Waiting for the mortal child to mature will take much longer than I want it to," Lucifer relented. "I shall recall Orin and my Legion and devise a new plan to accomplish the desires of my longing." As Lucifer summoned Orin and his Legion to come back down the abyssal to him, he sat on his earthly throne and waited for their appearance.

A demon apparated before him that Lucifer had not summoned. He was annoyed by this sudden appearance. "I did not ask for you to come and worship me! Why are you here?" Lucifer questioned in a tone that would strike fear in any demon's ears.

The demon bowed before his master and with trembling voice answered, "I have been bound and I suffered on the earthly plain, my lord. I wish to know how I have offended thee? Have I not proved to be a faithful servant?"

Having been uninterested in anything this demon might have said, Lucifer suddenly perked up and became interested in the appearance of the pesky demon. "Bound? Suffered? Explain your experience to me," Lucifer asked. Just then, in the same chamber as Lucifer and the uninvited demon, Ignis, and the Legion under Orin's command, appeared.

Lucifer's attention turned from the demon who had first appeared before him, and he spoke directly to Ignis. "Why do I wait for your commander to come before me, Fire?"

"I have no bearing on my commander, lord. He forced his plan and went to take the mortal child earlier than expected," Ignis told the story to Lucifer with as much fright as a child being forced to tell the truth.

"Early? He decided to enter the Dante child before we agreed?" Lucifer's voice boomed throughout the cathedral. Ignis, and the Legion that had been summoned by Lucifer, fell into immediate pain and torment. Lucifer's anger distracted him, and he did not block the suffering that could only be blocked by himself or while a demon was indwelling a mortal.

Lucifer regained his focus and repelled the anguish that his demons were suffering. With Ignis now regaining his focus from the torment he had been forced to endure, he glanced up at his master hoping that he had regained the ability to listen to him.

"Is the child now indwelled? Has Orin begun his journey to discover if this child will have the knowledge and ability the same as her father?"

Fearful of telling his lord the truth, Ignis knew he must, or face again what he just felt once Lucifer discovered he was lying. For a brief moment, Ignis thought to himself, "I am a creature that perpetuates many lies. Yet, here, before my master, I fear not telling the truth." "The mortal child hasn't been indwelled. I viewed from far off to see if my commander had indwelled it."

Expecting to be immediately thrust back into torment, Ignis kissed the cathedral ground that Lucifer once stood upon. He hoped this reverence might save him from torment this time.

Lucifer's words permeated into Ignis's demon mind, "Then, where is your commander?"

Ignis's words responded to his master's question with trembling conviction, "I do not know, my lord. He is gone and is bound from me."

Once again, the entire audience at Lucifer's call fell into pain and torment. And, once again, Lucifer released them from the suffering once his anger had subsided. Lucifer's gaze now focused on the demon who had first appeared before him. The demon shook uncontrollably and was in distress, but Lucifer called upon him. "You, demon, you decided to leave your host and come to me questioning my faithfulness to my subjects. How dare you appear before me with this blasphemy!"

Then, it occurred to Lucifer that this demon had mentioned that he was bound. Ignis had communicated the same word. He had not bound any of his angels on the earthly plain. He then moved over to the demon who cowered against the stark gray walls of his Cathedral, and just like he had done when he resurrected Demetri from his defeat at the hands of Gabriel, Lucifer's clammy finger stroked the demon as a father comforting a hurt child.

The demon quivered at this action by his master but had no choice but to allow it. "So, tell me my faithful servant, when you were bound, where were you?"

The demon, with sullen eyes and a reluctant mannerism, answered his master, "I was at a farm in the earthly region of Oregon." Lucifer's attention suddenly increased.

"Also, my lord, as I writhed in pain and felt my binding increase, I am certain I witnessed an angel, just like me, unbound on the other side of the gate."

Chapter 39:
Them Creeps

ALEX PULLED THE U-HAUL INTO THE DRIVEWAY of the 1940's Craftsman home that sat on a quiet tree lined street in Boulder, Colorado. This was their new home, and he was delighted that their journey to Colorado was over. He gazed at the Flatiron's which adorned the landscape and scenic views surrounding Boulder. Courtney had found this rental home on the internet, and they, together, had selected it sight-unseen.

Courtney pulled the car to the curb on the street in front of the house. She marveled at the trees and the sidewalk along the block of this older but well-maintained neighborhood. It was a far cry from the bungalow they had left in Astoria. Grabbing Annie from the back seat she rushed into the waiting arms of Alex. "If the inside is a great as the outside, we have definitely moved up!" Courtney excitedly offered.

As the Dante's moved up the steps to the front porch, Alex could not help but recall the memories of his childhood house. The front porch had a bench swing just like the one he used to sit in for hours. This time, he prayed he would witness no demons out on the front lawn seeking to study him.

The key to the front door was under a flower container, just like the landlord had told her, and Courtney unlocked and opened the door. The images that the landlord had sent did not do it justice. It was newly remodeled, but the owners had kept the charm of the wood trim and built-in cabinets that adorned the living room. Alex placed his arm around Courtney and the baby and, with a gleam on his face, proclaimed, "Great job, Court! Great job!"

The next few days were spent moving the few items they had brought with them from Oregon and doing furniture shopping. They had all their bedroom furniture along with Annie's crib and the baby's room furniture, so they decided to funnel their furniture budget towards a sectional sofa, and other living room items. The weekend had arrived, and they decided to celebrate the arrival at their new home by going out to dinner. It was not only a celebration of their new life together, but it was also Courtney's last days before starting her new position as head of nursing at the hospital.

As they enjoyed their exceptional meal at a local restaurant, they couldn't help but discuss the events that had unfolded in Idaho.

"Alex, I know you don't always like to talk about your experiences with the spirit world, but what happened in Idaho, happened to all of us," Courtney started the conversation.

"Yes, yes it did. I can't refute that," Alex responded.

Courtney, with careful thought, proceeded with the conversation by asking, "Why would that awful demon attack our little Annie? What was his reason? Also, what will happen to that demon? Can he try again?"

Alex held up one hand with his index finger extended, "Whoa, hold up there, girl. That's a lot of questions all at once."

"Sorry, sweetheart. It's just... I can't stop thinking about it. Our visit from Annabel Perkins, that terrible demon…everything," Courtney laid her heart out on the table.

"I can certainly understand why you're scared," Alex responded, while Annie Dante gazed in wonder at her parents. "This is what I know about that night. The demon was called, Orin. He had been stalking us, well, primarily me, for some time. I believe his plan was to indwell our little Annie, bide his time learning about me, believing that one day, when she was older, Annie would also have my abilities. He would possess her spirit and those abilities would belong to him. Then he would have all the answers to give to his master."

"Lucifer?" Courtney asked.

"Yep, Lucifer. You must give evil some credit. It was a dastardly plan. A long plan, but a dastardly one none the less."

Courtney looked over at Annabel and smiled as she responded, "Well, I'm not giving any credit to those creeps."

Alex had to laugh at Courtney's response. "As to your question about the whereabouts of the demon, Orin. He and his master were naïve to believe our God would let them have any child. They were deceived in their plan. Go figure, the great deceiver was deceived. A mighty Angel of the Lord, Michael, was sent to punish the demon and bind him until the day of judgement."

"Couldn't you have bound him?" Courtney questioned as she held onto every word her husband spoke.

"No, I don't have that ability. Only our God can bind Lucifer and his demons," Alex truthfully answered.

Courtney pondered his answers, but they only fueled more questions from her. "But didn't you bind Lucifer from Gayland's sanctuary? Isn't the demon world bound from that place?"

"Court, I am the keeper of God's will and providence. Our Lord has anointed me to be…what's the explanation

I'm looking for here…I am, and will be, in the Millennium of God's second coming, the jailer. I will have God's authority, accompanied by his host of heaven, to stand watch and guard over all who have been cast into bondage in the lake of fire. Until that time, any that come as a seeker against God's word and exploit their evil ways against that which God has made so, well, then I have his anointed power over them."

A tear was streaming down Courtney's cheek. Alex paid the check and walked his family out to their car to go home. To their new Colorado home.

"Those 'seekers' you mentioned, does that also include Satan?" Courtney asked her question, out of the blue, as they drove home.

"Yes, also Satan. I am a witness to Satan and his demons of what is to come and it ain't pretty. This will happen when Satan is allowed freedom here on earth after the Rapture when, our Lord, Jesus Christ, claims his bride, the Church, to come be with him." Alex replied with the confidence of the knowledge he had been given.

"So, until the rapture, you're the boss?" Courtney asked without trying to sound contrite.

"Yep, I'm the "boss" until the Rapture, after which Satan has his seven years to attempt to weave his evil plan. Then, with the Second Coming of our Lord, I become the 'boss' of all of them creeps again for the next one thousand years when they are cast into the lake of fire!"

Chapter 40:
One Soul for Another

IT HAD BEEN A RESTLESS NIGHT and Gary peered through squinting eyes at the dawns light breaking into the living room. He fumbled and knocked the empty glass that held the whiskey he drank the night before onto the floor. Luckily the glass didn't break, and he wouldn't have to sweep up the remains before Aspen found out. Then it dawned on him, his wife was gone and probably not coming home.

Stumbling into the bathroom, he parted with the previous days clothing and climbed into the shower to wash away the events of yesterday. Today would have to be much better. His beloved Shannon would be waiting for his arrival at the hospital and his future, once again, would be back on track.

As he drove to the hospital, Gary thought about how all his plans had changed. What were once plans with Aspen by his side were now the same plans but with Shannon standing beside him.

He walked down the sterile corridor of the hospital wing that held Shannon's room. Turning the corner, he was pleasantly surprised to see Shannon awake, sitting in a chair and not lying in bed, and fully dressed. "Wow, look at you!" Gary excitedly exclaimed.

Shannon, with a look that did not show relief or happiness that Gary had walked into the room, replied, "The doctors couldn't find any reason for my seizure. I've had a CT scan, blood tests, everything imaginable and they have no explanation for what happened to me. Shoot, I don't even remember anything. I barely remember arriving at Johnson's farm."

"Maybe it was just stress? I have probably put too much on your plate lately," Gary offered up his medical explanation.

"What about the farm? Did you get the inspection? Can you proceed with the city taking control?" Shannon asked but not fully showing a real interest in his answer.

Gary hung his head as he answered, not wanting to disappoint her. "No, after I was certain you were out of danger here at the hospital, I returned to the farm yesterday to go on the property. The Sheriff met me there. It seems the Trust Lawyer, Jim Turner, alerted him to our plan. Seems like the law says we can't enter the property without permission."

"Without permission? From whom?" Shannon questioned.

"The tenant. It appears Johnson has a distant relative that's living on the farm now," Gary answered.

Shannon's glare was not what Gary wanted to see from his beloved. "Distant relative? Who in the hell is this mystery person?"

"His name is Gayland Johnson. The Sheriff said he checks out. He's named in the Will that old man Johnson filed before his death. The Sheriff said he's living there now, and so, we must get permission from him to go on the property."

"Have you reached out to this Gayland Johnson yet?" Shannon pushed for an answer.

"Nobody's seen him. At least, not anybody local. Except the head of the Trust, who lives out of town."

Shannon stared out her hospital room window as she asked another question. "And who is this head of the Trust?"

"The guy's name is Alex Dante. Apparently, he used to live in Astoria, now he lives in Boulder, Colorado."

"Hmmm," Shannon replied turning her gaze back to Gary.

Gary strode forward and bent down next to the chair she was sitting in. Taking her hand in his, he looked into her distant eyes and began to pour out his heart. "Shannon, what you have wanted for some time now has happened. Aspen found out about us. She's left me. Now, we can be together without having to sneak around. I want you to be with me. When you leave this hospital, I will take care of you."

With an unprecedented smirk that was the last thing Gary expected, Shannon gave the least response to his statement that he thought he would receive from her. Shannon cast Gary's hand from hers like somebody throwing trash into the dumpster, "With everything that's happened in the last 24 hours, it's given me time to think. I don't want this anymore. I don't want you anymore. Somehow, none of this seems reasonable any longer."

Gary was stupefied. "Where is this coming from, Shannon? I know you've had a traumatic experience, perhaps you aren't thinking clearly."

"Actually, for the first time in a long time, I am thinking clearly. All the deceit, all the plotting and destroying people's lives, I don't want it any longer. You need to go ask for forgiveness from Aspen. You need to reconcile with her," Shannon confessed.

Gary felt sick. His body trembled at the words spoken to him. "But what about us?" He desperately implored.

An older man, with a medium build walked into the room. His hair had grey highlights around the temples, and he walked over to where Gary, who was now standing, stood weak and confused. Extending a hand towards Gary and offering a handshake, the man spoke. "Hello, I'm Nick Brown. I'm Shannon's father."

Gary responded by limply shaking the man's hand although he did not reply with any verbal greeting. Nick Brown realized he must have arrived at an awkward time. Turning towards where Shannon was sitting, her father spoke. "You're all checked out, Shannon. Ready to go home?"

Gary looked first at Shannon and then towards her father and with a shaking sound in his voice asked, "Home? Home to your apartment? You didn't need to bother your father to take you home. I could've done that."

Shannon looked at Gary with sympathetic eyes. Eyes he had never seen from her. Her eyes always showed fire and desire for him. This time, he was convinced her eyes showed pity.

"She's coming home with her mother and me. I appreciate everything you've done for my girl, young man, but it's time for her to come home."

"Where…where is home, Shannon?" Gary asked in desperate need of an answer.

"She's coming home to Nebraska," Nick Brown replied.

As Gary watched the woman who, until recently, spurred his political ambitions, along with his physical desires, drive away with her father, he felt lost. For the first time since he could remember, everything hadn't gone his way. He was so used to winning. This experience was foreign to him, and he longed for answers. His arrogance and lack of morals had ruined his future.

He returned to his home. The thought of going into the office today was something he couldn't fathom. The memories that office held for him would only be nightmares for him now. He sat down in the same chair that had served as his bed last night. He picked up his cell phone and dialed Aspen's number. The voice on the phone informed him that it was a number that was no longer in service. Shannon's last wish for Gary was to reconcile with his wife. With no way to reach her, that was now out of the question.

Gary walked into the kitchen and searched for any liquor he could find. He found an almost full bottle of vodka. He wasn't sure how old the bottle was, but he didn't care. He didn't bother to grab another glass and simply started taking gulps straight out of the bottle. As he drank, he couldn't help but think about Shannon and what had changed. She was a different person today from the one he knew yesterday. Something had changed with her. What was once a confident, aggressive woman, was suddenly gone.

"What the hell happened to her?" Gary pondered as the alcohol began to work on his coherence. He stumbled to his bedroom and into the closet. Fumbling on a shelf above his clothes hanging neatly on hangers that had been the handy work of his lost wife, Aspen, he found the case he was searching for.

Gary struggled with the clips that held the black case shut but was finally able to get it open. Inside laid a .38 Special revolver that was fully loaded but had never been fired. He grabbed the gun and returned to his living room and what was left of the bottle of Vodka sitting on the table next to his chair. He picked up the bottle and drained the last remaining drops inside it.

Stroking the handle of the gun as if it were a lover, Gary admired the revolver. It served as protection for his family. His precious family, should they be threatened by an intruder looking to do harm. He tilted his head back on the headrest of the chair and stared at a blurry ceiling.

Moving the barrel of the gun up to his mouth he inserted it in and past his tongue. At that moment, Gary had no knowledge that he and his family had been threatened by an intruder, even though they had.

This was not an intruder who had happened upon them as it passed through the town of La Grande. This was an intruder that was not of flesh and blood. One that was least expected or realized. Gary pulled back the hammer of the revolver and slowly pulled the trigger. Images flashed through his mind. Raising the trophy of his High School State Championship, kissing Aspen at the altar at their wedding.

Those images faded. Gary was standing before the evil one and faced an eternity that could have been avoided had he not chosen this path. The soul that had existed within the physical body that once was Gary Harding now began to writhe with pain. The demon who had abandoned Shannon Brown and decided to retreat down the abyssal was also present along with Ignis and his earthly infantry of evil. The demon laughed when he realized that the damage that could have been done by his releasing one soul, the female host, simply led another soul to be delivered to his master. This situation could not have worked out better for the demon's situation.

Lucifer commanded this new soul to rescind further into the pit of hell. Once Gary's soul had disappeared from the evil audience that had been watching his soul disappear into oblivion, Lucifer turned his attention back to the demon that had come uninvited. "So, tell me angel, are you certain there was another like you inside the barrier to which you were denied entry?"

"Yes, master, I am certain," the demon responded.

Ignis now addressed Lucifer, seeking to ask his master for guidance. "Lord, shall I return to earth to attempt to discover where my commander, Orin, is?"

Expecting Lucifer to be annoyed at his question, Ignis was surprised by the relative calm his master displayed. Waving his hand at Ignis, Lucifer replied, "No, I am well aware of where Orin is held. I put him there. It is his punishment for disobeying me and embarking on his fruitless plan too early. I will deal with Orin myself. Now go, return to your sanctuary, and enjoy my reward to all of you. I will call for you when you are needed."

It was not out of character for Satan to deceive his angels. He was a master at deception.

Ignis and the other demons showed no haste in venturing back up the pathway. Lucifer's benevolence was not questioned by any of them.

The uninvited demon, still trembling with fear of his master, timidly asked, "And me, lord, what is to become of me?"

Lucifer delayed his answer for a moment and then replied in a calm manner, "You will take me up your pathway. The same pathway by which you came to me. Then you will accompany me to the barrier where you witnessed the angel inside that to which you were denied."

The demon, along with his master, departed the chamber, and with supernatural speed arrived at the portal near Johnson's farm in La Grande, Oregon. Despite the failure of Orin, and the need to find the traitor, Gayland, Lucifer knew, at the core of his evil being, that this lowly angel, who was nothing to him, had stumbled onto the gem of his longing.

Chapter 41: Exposure

Tyler handed the metal trays to Cindy who placed them under the running water of the kitchen sink. She plopped the metal piece that formed the individual ice cubes into the liquid water and walked each tray over to the freezer section of the new refrigerator. Opening the freezer door she slid the trays neatly into the bottom of the freezer section. There was nothing else to put in the freezer, so the ice trays had plenty of room.

Cindy turned towards Tyler and glanced up and down, side to side, as if she was looking for something. "Listen, Gayland, this appliance is as quiet as a mouse and will last for years. In a few hours you will be back in the ice business." Cindy called out to an invisible demon that she had no idea where he was.

Gayland studied Cindy intently. She was truly a mortal he found intriguing. After all, she triumphed over the mighty Demetri and that was the domino that fell to expose Alex Dante's power. Secretly, he feared her. Her alabaster eyes alone were haunting.

His ignorance and lack of human knowledge regarding the box that produced his beloved ice had led to his anxiety and fear that he might never again experience that mortal delight. He realized that most of what he had been feeling was caused by his lack of faith that Alex Dante would continue to deliver on his promises. He understood that the appearance of these mighty agents of Alex and Gabriel's God were proof that he should no longer fear his situation.

With this realization, Gayland made a calculated decision. Even though these mortals could not see him, he had the ability to expose his presence to them. Doing so could be dangerous but, somehow, he felt he could trust them.

Tyler motioned to Cindy that perhaps it was time for them to depart and leave this demon to his peace. Cindy was more than willing to comply with her husband's decision. She had really had enough of being at this farmhouse to last a lifetime. Just as Tyler and Cindy were moving towards the front screen door, they both saw an apparition near the front of the screen door. At first, it was just a blur, like a figure walking in a deep fog.

Cindy held tightly onto Tyler's left arm. In her mind she knew what was coming. Slowly, the image became clearer to the couple and the blurry outlines became focused and sharp. Tyler marveled at the specter before them. Despite understanding that this was a demon that had once communed with Satan, he found Gayland magnificent.

Gayland stood before them clad in his mortal persona of Farmer Johnson's attire adorned with a black leather motorcycle jacket over the ensemble. "As you are a man of the cloth representing Gabriel's God, I am sure my appearance is a bit startling?" Gayland offered being sure that both Tyler and Cindy were astonished.

Tyler fumbled for the words to reply. "Ah... yes, I suppose. We didn't expect to see you today, Gayland."

Cindy had let go of Tyler's arm and moved closer to where Gayland was standing. This unexpected movement made him uncomfortable.

"Why do you retreat, Gayland? It is obvious my approach makes you uncomfortable."

"Forgive me, girl with the alabaster eyes. I mean you no disrespect." Gayland replied, as a knight might say to a Queen as he is being presented to the Royal Court.

"Is that what you call me? The girl with the alabaster eyes?" Cindy earnestly asked the demon.

"Your mortal eyes are intriguing and mysterious. I meant it with all respect and reverence."

Cindy looked back towards Tyler, whose jaw had finally closed, and smiled with great glee. "Look, honey, a demon. Now you have seen what Alex and I have seen."

"Lucky me," Tyler smugly responded.

Tyler had longed for a closer examination of the spirit world. As a Pastor, he was well aware of the existence of other created beings and he always hoped for a better understanding of Angels and demons, but this was beyond anything he could have hoped for.

Gayland stood still and quiet before them. He had never appeared before mortals before unless it was to wreak havoc and malice. "I did not want you to leave my sanctuary without me showing my gratitude for restoring my frozen water." This statement was odd and had never come from his demon mouth before. "I know you are mighty agents of Alex Dante. The fact that he would summon you here, to my sanctuary, to restore this pleasure to me, is, well..." Gayland had no words to finish his thought.

"Benevolent, truthful." Cindy offered to complete Gayland's sentence.

Gayland, who was completely at a loss for words could only reply, "Perhaps."

The cat had come onto the scene and proceeded over to brush up against Cindy's leg. The same leg that held the scar from her bout with Demetri. She picked up the cat and stroked it around its ears.

"Mice are not quiet," Gayland said.

"What?" Cindy replied.

"You had spoken about my new mortal box that makes my frozen water being as quiet as a mouse," Gayland rebutted.

Cindy chuckled, as it seemed odd to be in a humorous conversation with a being that existed to destroy her kind. "It's a saying. One you wouldn't understand."

The cat jumped from Cindy's arms and walked over to Gayland and brushed up against his legs. Gayland picked the cat up and both Tyler and Cindy were amazed the cat allowed this demon to do so without resistance.

"It catches mice for its mortal sustenance. Therefore, I suspect that mice are not quiet," Gayland offered as a scientist with a new discovery.

Cindy and Tyler both shook their heads in agreement to the demon's statement.

Tyler couldn't resist in engaging Gayland in deeper questions about the demon world and his present situation. Because his guests had been gracious and respectful, Gayland did his best to answer Tyler. Once the conversation seemed to have begun to annoy Gayland, Tyler realized all the answers to the evil universe could not be asked and answered today. Plus, Tyler realized it was getting late in the day.

"We have completed the task that our friend Alex has asked of us, and now we will respectfully leave you, Gayland, to live in your sanctuary in peace." Tyler offered, trying not to provoke any feelings that the demon might have that they had worn out their welcome.

With that statement from Tyler, Gayland was suddenly gone. All that existed in the space he had once stood was

the cat, licking his paw. As the couple moved out of the
farmhouse, across the creaking wooden porch, and out to
their car, Tyler noticed the cat had appeared on the porch
standing next to a rocking chair that was moving with
seemingly nothing to propel it.

"Should we have taken the cat?" Cindy asked as Tyler
placed the car in reverse to back up.

With one arm on the steering wheel and his head
looking out over his right shoulder to get a better view of
his backing direction, Tyler answered, "That cat is home.
This is where it belongs. It reminds Gayland of the place
he came from before he trusted the wrong god."

Suddenly, Tyler stopped the SUV. Looking out over
his right shoulder, he saw a bright flash of light close by. It
couldn't have been lightning because there wasn't a cloud
in the sky.

Chapter 42:
Truth Surrounds

THE AIR IN BOULDER HAD BEGUN TO TURN CRISP with the Fall season. Fall was different here in Colorado than what the Dante's were accustomed to. Courtney pulled off her jacket as she entered the front room of their home. "I almost didn't take my jacket this morning. It was quite warm. Now, I'm glad I did because it's freezing out there!" Courtney announced as she let go a shiver that came from the inner most part of her body.

"I don't think we're in Kansas anymore, Toto," Alex laughingly said.

"The hospital's quite busy. We're short at least three nurses and that's below minimum. My attention is almost exclusively on interviewing candidates. It's a far cry from just worrying about making my med rounds," Courtney explained as though this was a revelation only now being exposed.

Alex smiled as he replied, "This is what you signed up for. They certainly pay you enough to make me a kept man, so, buck up girl."

Courtney walked over to where Annabel was laying on a blanket and picked her up and brought her to her shoulder. Kissing the child on her forehead, Courtney spoke to her in a childlike manner, "My poor baby. Did this mean ole man ignore you all day?"

Alex laughed and replied, "Of course I did. With what you pay me, I do as little as possible." They chuckled at the interchange between them, and Alex offered that spaghetti and homemade Italian meatballs were on the menu for the night.

"Garlic bread, too?" Courtney asked.

"Of course, I'm Italian," Alex smugly commented.

She walked over to where her husband was sitting and kissed him on the cheek. "I love you, my Italian man."

The evening dinner conversation centered around Courtney's journey in her new position. All the struggles, but also the excitement and pleasure she was discovering, being the boss. "How about you, Alex, when do you start school?"

"Next Monday. I meet with the Dean to chart my journey to being Dr. Dante," Alex responded.

Courtney was pleased that Alex was staying the course and beginning his studies and all the work that would be required to meet his goal in life. "Are you still comfortable with the Nanny we chose for Annie?" Courtney asked as she sipped a glass of Chianti.

"Yes, I think so. She's a believer and that's important. She's young, but at least we don't have to be concerned that she could bring one of those creeps with her."

Courtney agreed with Alex's evaluation. Since the experience they had in Boise, both parents desired to surround themselves with mortal believers. They understood that God had supplied the Heavenly Host to protect them but having that barrier between themselves and Lucifer's group was important.

As the night proceeded, all was calm and tranquil. Courtney had carried a sleeping Annabel back to her crib and rejoined her husband in the living room. Alex was scanning the course guide that he would be hurled into on

Monday next, and Courtney picked up a novel that she had been endeavoring to read.

Suddenly, Alex's body indicated he was on high alert. Courtney noticed it immediately. "Honey, what is it? Is Annie in danger?" Courtney excitedly asked.

"No, Annie is fine. I just sense something. It's different than anything I've ever sensed before." Alex responded.

"What do you sense? Tell me, please," Courtney implored.

Alex tilted his head to stare directly into the kitchen. Standing in the kitchen, next to the small table where they eat their meals, was the Angel, Gabriel. Not in the persona of the overweight George Billingham, but in all the majesty of the mighty Angel of God that he was.

Alex came to his feet and, without acknowledging Courtney's exasperation to know what he was seeing and doing, he walked into the kitchen and the presence of the mighty Angel.

"Dear Alex, I understand you would prefer to see me as my mortal persona, George, but I am here tonight to protect you and your family. This requires me to be my spiritual creature."

The beauty and radiance that emitted from Gabriel astonished Alex. "Then this is serious, isn't it?" Alex inquired.

"Yes, my friend. I am here to prevent you from traveling to where the evil one desires you to come."

"I'm confused, Gabriel. Lucifer will summon me?" Alex asked in total confusion.

"No, he is not able to summon you. He desires your presence."

Gabriel waved his hand to display a scene in front of Alex. It was absolutely the most vivid virtual reality that Alex had ever seen. It was also the most alarming. He recognized it immediately. It was Gayland's farm.

There, in the scene that Gabriel displayed for him, Alex could see figures moving. It became clear to him that what he was seeing was Tyler and Cindy. They were standing at the gate entrance to the farm. Clearly, he could also see that Gayland was standing with them. Alex gasped at the scene.

"I have put my friends in danger! Satan is there! He has discovered Gayland's sanctuary! I must go!"

The scene disappeared from Alex's sight. Gabriel spoke with authority and power. "This is the reason I come before you tonight. You shall not go! Satan has no power here. Yes, he is angry at the demon that betrayed him, but the boundary defined at this farm is Truth. Satan cannot enter Truth. He refuses to recognize it. The demon Gayland has drunk the elixir of the Truth. He is protected."

"Yes…but what of Tyler and Cindy?" Alex asked with anxiety building to a crescendo like a symphony orchestra.

"Alex, Tyler is a deliverer of the Truth. Cindy has been delivered to the Truth. You said earlier that you wish to surround you and your family with mortals that know the Truth," Gabriel spoke to the answer that Alex had already been given.

"You were here to hear that, weren't you?" Alex confirmed.

"Then understand that your friends are well equipped in this battle. Lucifer desires your presence. He will believe he has killed two birds with one stone. The great deceiver will come to understand that his arrogance deceives him."

"Then I will stay with my family. Praise be to our Lord, Jesus Christ," Alex confirmed.

With that statement, Gabriel left Alex's presence. Alex knew he was still there, but he should pray for what was about to occur. As he fell to his knees, an impatient Courtney walked to his side, knelt with her husband, and grabbed him by the hand. "I don't know what just happened. I trust that God is in control. I will pray with you, Alex."

Chapter 43: Satan Arrives

Tyler quickly released his seatbelt and with one leg out of the car and the other holding the door, looked back to where he had seen the flash of light. Cindy exited the car and quickly moved to the side of the car where Tyler stood. An uneasy feeling engulfed her. She was alarmed at her husband's abrupt stopping of the car and stepping out of it, but she was even more alarmed by the concerned look on his face.

Cindy quickly glanced back to the farmhouse. She was uncertain why the house attracted her glance but once her look had scanned the house, she placed her hand on Tyler's sleeve and directed his stare away from the boundary of the farm and back to the farmhouse. Tyler was shocked to see the physical body of Gayland slowly moving down the steps of the porch and towards them.

Both Cindy and Tyler could see that the focus of Gayland's attention was not on them but pierced right through them and out onto the horizon beyond the property gate. The look on Gayland's face was not pleasant. He walked past the couple, who were standing by their car, and stopped directly at the old, rusted gate that, once opened, would lead off the property, and out into the mortal world.

"What is he staring at? Did he see the same flash of light that I saw?" Tyler inquired of Cindy like a man desperate for answers to a crossword puzzle.

"I believe he sees much more than a flash of light. Something, or someone, is coming," Cindy replied with angst.

Gayland stood as still as a statue. His gaze was locked in beyond the gate like a hunter sitting in a blind who had spotted his prey. It had been a short period of time since Tyler had seen the flash of light and Gayland had walked to the gate when Gayland began to speak in a human voice. "I see you have discovered my sanctuary. I did not doubt that eventually you would find it. And me."

Standing at the outside of the gate, Lucifer had appeared in his physical form before the demon, Gayland, and the humans on the other side. "I see you prefer the company of mortals versus your own kind."

"I find their mortality a breath of fresh air," Gayland rebutted.

Lucifer glanced past Gayland, focusing on Tyler and Cindy. He returned his gaze back to Gayland. "Hmm, I see. But these are creatures whose immortal souls belong to Gabriel's God. They are not available for you to capture for me."

"I am no longer your instrument for perdition," Gayland replied with all the courage he could summon.

Lucifer stroked his beardless chin which was his mannerism whenever he was being challenged. "Yes, perhaps so, Gayland, but you made your choice a long time ago. Their immortality is not available to you, just as their souls are not available for me. If you had wanted to enjoy human pleasures, like the fluid you consume, why did you not just ask me? I would have allowed it."

Tyler looked over at Cindy with a frightened but, at the same time, stern look on his face. "Can you hear this? Who, or what, is Gayland talking to?"

Cindy, with a timid and reserved manner replied, "I believe it is sin in the flesh. I feel that Satan is near and at the gate." Tyler shuddered at his wife's revelation.

Lucifer paced back and forth in front of the gate. Sometimes staring at the ground and then bringing his eyes back up to look at Gayland. The demon who had led Satan to Gayland's sanctuary cowered behind his master. It wanted no part of this meeting.

Gayland, in a sarcastic manner, offered up a reply and followed it with a question for his former master. "The liquid has proved to be more than a human pleasure. It opened my eyes to the understanding that what you just offered would have been a lie. Just like all you offered before it. Why do you choose to come to me? It serves no purpose for you to waste your time with me."

"Perhaps, yes, you are a distraction. Still, you are not a distraction to Dante. He somehow finds purpose in your existence," Lucifer acknowledged. Turning his gaze past Gayland and towards Cindy, Lucifer pointed at her and spoke, "Ah, the girl with the alabaster eyes. What a prize she would have been."

Tyler's fear had turned to obstinance as he called out to Gayland and implored him to share with them the conversation he was having. Gayland relayed Satan's comments about Cindy, and Lucifer's comment, like an arrow striking directly at her past, irritated Tyler. He felt secure enough to call out directly to the evil one, even though he could not see him. "Be gone, evil one! You have no authority here."

Satan had grown equally tired and irritated since his arrival at Gayland's sanctuary. He did not care for these believers in Gabriel's God, and he didn't want to carry on any banter with them. Deciding to ask the question he sought to ask from the very first moment he arrived to confront Gayland, he demanded, "One of you needs to summon your master, Alex Dante. Be it you, Gayland, or your human friends. He will show me the respect I deserve and allow me to enter."

"Ah, so you admit it now. You believe Alex has bound you from here. The mighty king of perdition must appeal to a mere mortal for entrance," Gayland fired the cannon shot at the heart of his former master.

Lucifer was clearly angry at Gayland's response. "Dante must remove the barrier and allow me to claim my own. You are my angel, and he must allow me to claim you! You provide no advantage for him, coward. You have defiled my faith and you are mine. You are a traitor, and I demand retribution!"

Suddenly, Gayland became afraid and terrified. Not at the words that were spoken by Lucifer, but because the cat had squeezed through the gate and, with his bottom on the ground and its two front paws resting directly in front of Satan, stared up at the manifestation in front of him and let out a loud and obnoxious "meow".

Gayland feared that Lucifer could harm the animal. He wasn't sure that he could or would. He was almost sure that a cat had never presented itself before the evil one. Cindy had also become alarmed at the sight of the cat on the outside of the gate. Much like Gayland, she feared that Satan might harm the animal.

Clearly distracted by the appearance of the animal, Satan swung his right foot towards the body of the cat with a kicking action. Having missed his mark, the cat let out a ferocious "HISS", sprang up on its hind legs and with one of his front paws, extended his claws out and embedded them into the leg of Satan, which had been exposed from beneath the robes he wore. Gayland was amused that a spiritual being, such as the master he had once worshiped, could suffer a wound from a simple, feral farm cat.

The cat quickly retreated through the gate and returned to the protection of the demon, Gayland. Satan reached his mortal manifested hand down to rub the wound on his leg that had been administered by the wrath of one of God's creatures.

Cindy and Gayland couldn't help but laugh at what had just happened. She was certain that the cat had bested the personification of pure evil and blurted out a response, "I wouldn't expect it to bring you a mouse to share for dinner, either!"

A red hue appeared in Lucifer's eyes as he spoke to Gayland. "If you won't summon Dante to face me, then it is because he is weak. He fears me. You know it is only a matter of time until his protection will be lifted from you, and then I will have my revenge."

"Then, I will wait for that time to come. I have always known this peace will not last forever," Gayland reluctantly replied.

Then, Cindy spoke the words that turned the tide of this supernatural meeting. "Satan, why are you obsessed with Gayland? He has received the Truth, and that Truth is that Jesus Christ is Lord. It is too late for him, but do you not realize, it is also too late for you? The Son of Man is coming, and you will have your brief time, here on earth, to try and convince mortals that you are worthy to be worshipped. Leave this creature alone and go make haste to complete your deception. Your obsession with this demon, who turned against you, only fogs your future. Do not tarry. Be gone from here!"

It pained Lucifer to hear the wisdom of this mortal woman. He would never admit it. Especially not to Gayland. His energy must be used to control and prepare the man that would make the world succumb to his demands and worship him as God. His time was growing near, and the folly to have pursued the coward, Gayland, had only served to delay and distract him.

Gayland turned from the rusting gate to face Tyler and Cindy who stood in disbelief of what had just happened. "He has left." Gayland said in a deadpan manner. "I do not know whose words cast him away. I am certain that you do not have the same powers as Alex Dante, but the powers you both possess are very strong."

Gayland picked up the cat and walked past Tyler and Cindy on his way back to the porch that held the very elixir of his existence. Shortly after he reached the screen door to the farmhouse and entered it, Cindy could hear the cracking of ice as it fell from the metal tray.

Tyler and Cindy decided that their time with the demon, Gayland, must end. Everything Tyler had yearned for, and was secretly jealous of Alex for, had come true today. He wasn't sure if he would ever see Gayland again, but his faith and strength in God surged inside him.

Having passed through the metal gate, Tyler closed it and wrapped the rusty metal chain around the post that held it shut. A small grin appeared on Tyler's face as he could read the sign on the gate that read "NO TRESPASSING".

Chapter 44:
Celebration

Seven years later

"HURRY, ANNIE. We mustn't be late picking up your father," Courtney pushed her daughter along like cattle being herded for branding.

"I'm coming, Mom. I can't find my shoes," Annabel Dante explained with an anguished response. Coming out of her bedroom and hopping from one foot to the other, Annabel managed to find, and put on, her shoes.

Courtney was in the living room putting on her coat. She grabbed a coat for Annabel and handed it to her daughter. "C'mon, Annie. Dad is going to be standing in the cold wondering where we are."

Looking at the young boy of four years old standing next to a petite woman, Annabel pleaded with her mother. "Can't George and Jessica come, too? Dad wants this celebration to be the whole family and leaving Jess and Georgie out just doesn't seem right."

Jessica had served the Dante family for the last seven years as the nanny for Annabel and George. Since they moved to Boulder, the kids had never known another nanny and Jessica had been instrumental in helping Courtney when George was born. Annabel was very fond of Nanny Jessica and to any observant person, they would see that Jessica loved Annabel and George.

Jessica grabbed George's hand and walked to the front door where Courtney was attempting to induce her daughter to walk out. "Hey, George and I are having pizza. We have a way better deal than you girls. Besides, your daddy wants a special night out with his girls." Jessica said trying to temper the idea that had popped into Annabel's mind.

Courtney mouthed the words, "thank you" towards Jessica and hurried Annabel out the door. Once inside the car, Courtney looked in her rear-view mirror and noticed Annabel was deep in thought. "Don't you just love all the Christmas lights?" Courtney asked, hoping to bring her daughter's attention back to conversation.

"I do. The lights are so pretty," Annabel quickly answered but showed no sign of engaging her mother in additional chat.

"What are you so deep in thought about, baby?" Courtney inquired.

"Mom, are we moving?" Annabel blurted out in a surprising manner.

Not wanting to endanger both by taking her eyes off the road, Courtney pulled the car over to look at Annabel in the back seat.

"Move? Where in the world did you get that idea, honey?"

"I heard daddy say the other night that he should probably give some man in Oregon the first chance for a place for daddy to work at," Annabel innocently answered her mother.

Courtney smiled at Annabel and let out a little chuckle. Feeling the need to settle the angst that Annie was feeling, she gave the best answer she could come up with. "Sweetie, daddy was joking about an old promise to our old boss in

Oregon. That man doesn't expect your daddy to move to Oregon. Daddy and I are staying put. Here in Colorado."

"Good! I don't think Georgie wants to leave either. Not to mention Jessica. She has a boyfriend!" Annabel honestly replied.

"Well then, it's settled. We're all Coloradans." Courtney laughed. Sometimes she was amazed at just how intuitive Annabel Dante was.

Then, as Courtney entered the road once again, thinking that the intense questions of her daughter had been asked, Annabel fired another question. "So is daddy a real doctor tomorrow?"

Glancing back at her daughter, Courtney was uncertain of the meaning of the question. "What do you mean 'is daddy a real Doctor tomorrow'?"

"Well, we're going to celebrate tonight at the restaurant because you said that daddy is officially a doctor. That's what you said. So, does that mean he's a real doctor now?" Annabel, with all the mystery of innocence, asked.

Courtney took a moment to collect her thoughts before she answered. "Annie, daddy has been a real doctor for the last fourteen months. His working at the hospital was just so other doctors could, you know, look over his shoulder until he was comfortable being a doctor. Now he's comfortable and those people that looked over his shoulder believe so, too."

Annabel gazed out her car window after receiving the information her mother gave her. Looking back towards the front of the car where her mom was driving, Annabel replied, "I love Christmas lights."

The mind of a child fascinated Courtney. She pulled the car into a side entrance of the hospital and within seconds, Alex exited the doors and walked towards the car. Courtney turned off the engine and exited the driver's side of the car and walked toward the rear. She met Alex there and handed him the keys, expecting he wanted to drive.

'No, you drive tonight, Court. I want to talk with my favorite girl in the back seat," Alex laughingly poked at his wife.

Courtney let out a false pout but then hugged her husband and gave him a quick peck on his lips. She brought one hand to his face where she noticed the years were showing the salt and pepper appearing in what was once jet-black hair. The goatee he now sported on his face showed the same degree of aging.

"With your beard, you look like a psychiatrist." Courtney teased her husband.

"Well, I am one." Alex smugly replied. He opened the passenger door and poked his head into the car. "There's my favorite girl!" Alex offered with true joy in his voice.

"Congratulations on becoming a real doctor, daddy," Annabel replied.

Alex climbed into the car and reaching to put his seatbelt on, gave Courtney a puzzled look regarding Annabel's speech. Courtney simply shrugged at the wonderment her husband displayed on his face and offered, "I'll fill you in later."

As the Dante's traveled to the restaurant where they would have their celebratory meal, Courtney took the chance that Annabel was preoccupied with the lights of the season and she could attempt a more adult conversation with her husband. "So, did you give the hospital staff an answer?" Courtney quizzed.

"I did. I'm taking two weeks, then, on the psychiatric wing of St. Andrews, in a medical office on the sixth floor, a placard will appear on a door," Alex answered.

"And what will that placard read?" Courtney asked, fully knowing the answer.

"Dr. A. Dante, Psychiatrist and Keeper of the Demons" Alex replied, with all humor exposed in his answer.

"I know you carefully weighed the offer from the University. Being a professor was something you never thought you'd be interested in, but I know you have changed, my dear husband."

Alex smiled as he studied the lines of Courtney's face. The last years had displayed the fact that both were growing older, but to Alex, she was as beautiful today as ever. "Just too many demons running around campus for me to consider teaching."

"You never told me that there are demons at school?" Courtney questioned.

"Lots of them. I just didn't want to alarm you. After Boise, I felt you had experienced enough demons for a lifetime," Alex revealed.

"Are there demons indwelling the students?" Courtney pushed one more question at her husband.

Alex could only answer with honesty. "There are just as many indwelling the professors. Satan's using them to change the tide and condition their hearts towards hate for those of us that believe in Jesus Christ."

Sensing that this was neither the time nor place to continue this conversation, Alex boasted, "Tonight is a celebration! A celebration of daddy becoming a real doctor!"

Alex carried a sleeping Annabel in his arms. Once inside the house he placed her in her bed and kissed her on the forehead as he placed the covers over her. Walking to the slightly open door that led to George's room, Alex peeked inside to see his boy deep into slumber. Having named his son after the greatest friend and Angel he had ever known, the proud father retreated to the living room where Courtney was expressing her gratitude and good night wishes to Jessica.

"She is such a blessing," Courtney acknowledged.

"Yes, she truly is," Alex replied with a yawn.

Courtney realized it had been a long day for her husband and didn't want to prolong his journey to getting some much-needed sleep, but she stopped him before he could retreat down the hallway to their bedroom. "Real quick, come into the kitchen. I have something to show you before you go to bed. It's a special present," Courtney prodded.

Complying with the wishes of his wife, Alex trudged reluctantly into the kitchen. It wasn't that he wanted to discount her kindness in getting him a present, it was just that he needed to sleep. There, on the kitchen table, sat a gift bag with colorful writing that read, "Congratulations!"

With a smile on his face, Alex opened the bag and pulled out the contents there within. Coming to his side, Courtney placed an arm around the waist of her husband and kissed him on the cheek. "It's an old school coffee percolator. They seem to be making a comeback," she said, with all the excitement of a schoolgirl who had met her first best friend.

Alex twirled the box from side to side as he admired the surprise that had just been revealed. He placed the box down on the kitchen table, hugged Courtney and gave her a kiss that displayed how much he cared for this woman. He released her to admire the gift once again. "I've missed my coffee maker. I'm so grateful to God to have you, my love!"

Playfully pushing her husband towards the hallway and towards their bedroom, Courtney exclaimed, "You had better get some sleep. George, aka, the Angel Gabriel, will probably be sitting at our kitchen table waiting for his morning cup!"

"No doubt," Alex laughed.

As the couple slid into bed and Courtney moved over to place herself in the comfortable embrace of her husband, she added one more bit of news before he drifted off to sleep. "Oh, I forgot to mention, Cindy and Tyler called to wish you congratulations."

Mumbling, Alex replied with a sleepy tone, "That's nice."

"Oh yeah, Cindy's pregnant. They hope to get lucky with this third one and have a boy!"

Suddenly, Alex was wide awake with eyes the size of Kennedy half dollars.

Chapter 45:
The Abomination

HAVING MADE HIS CHOICE, LUCIFER REVELED in his decision. There had been so many to choose from and this man was his choice. It had been centuries since he had plotted, planned, and sought this man who would become him, in the flesh. The time to indwell a human had come and it would be him that would do it. The events of the world, the condemnation of those who believed in Gabriel's God, all revealed that this was the time, and this was the man.

Charisma exuded from this man. All those who knew him were delighted by his compassion, understanding and ability to solve any problem that confronted those that were the leaders of the One World Order. He was a politician's politician. The man who would become Lucifer in the flesh operated the floor of the governing body to which he had been elected, as an expert in human relations.

With every alliance this politician formed with those leaders that wanted to propel their agenda, Lucifer felt more and more that this man was like his son. He laughed at the thought. Then, a sobering idea came to him, "why not?" He rejoiced in the knowledge that his plan would be the same as Gabriel's God devised to use his son to exalt him, as God of the Universe. Except this time, it would work better. Simply duplicating the Holy Trinity that so many humans had foolishly bought into was not copying, this time it would work, it would be better, and this time, he would prove he was the one to be worshipped as God.

The meeting of the governments that were forming the One World Order was called to order. His choice, the man who would soon become the antichrist, was nominated to be in a leadership role, but not the leader. Lucifer knew that his son's position would soon change. After the meeting was adjourned and the man who would become the antichrist resigned to his office, accompanied only by an assistant who served as his right-hand man, Lucifer made his move. First, he empowered the assistant with supernatural powers. Powers that were created out of pure evil and sin. This man, with the use of miracles, would create the environment for his boss to ascend to the rank of leader of the governments that formed the One World Order.

Lucifer indwelled the man. As he consumed every fiber of humanity that this man had only just a few moments ago possessed, the man who was now Satan's son, the antichrist, lost all humanity. With his indwelling, Lucifer lost all concern over what Gabriel's God had planned for the mysterious mortal, Alex Dante. Dante and his purpose no longer had meaning to him. He would now focus on using his son to gain what he had always needed, which was to be God. He would deal with the traitor, Gayland, to which he already had a plan, when that time came. For now, he must remove every obstacle that the followers of Gabriel's God placed in his way.

The antichrist and his assistant tilted their glasses, filled with an unknown spirit, towards each other. With the clink of their glasses completed, they both took a drink and toasted the abomination that was coming.

Chapter 46:
Red As Human Blood

GAYLAND ROCKED IN HIS CHAIR. The cat that rested on his demon lap had become accustomed to spending more and more time in that position. Not understanding mortal time, not only for humans, but also for the creatures that inhabited this earthly plain, Gayland considered that the age of this animal was taking its toll. He tolerated the animal and the time it wanted to spend in relaxation. This animal had stood up to his former master, and for that reason had earned the respect and reverence of Gayland. Never wanting to have mortal companions since coming to what was now truly his sanctuary, the demon considered that if he had to have a mortal friend, then this animal was his only choice. In the emptiness of his demon soul, he began to reconcile that he was glad the cat was there.

Sipping a fresh batch of iced tea, Gayland looked off into the winter sky, out onto the horizon. It had been years since he paid much attention to the white orb that appeared in the night sky, but this time, as dusk brought forward the darkness that inhabited the night, he noticed the orb wasn't white or emitting light as it normally did. This time, it was red. Red as human blood.

Chapter 47:
Promise

"C'MON DADDY, WE NEED TO CATCH UP to mommy and Annie." George excitedly barked at his father.

"I'm coming, George. Hold your horses!" Alex barked back at his energetic son.

"But daddy, I don't have any horses." George answered with confusion.

"Never mind, never mind," Alex exclaimed as a man wanting to drop the subject. As Alex and George finally caught up to Courtney and Annabel, Alex stopped in awe, looking at the valley down below them. Despite being the winter season, the Colorado sun was warm and made a family hike in the foothills above Boulder a desirable family event. The valley was still covered in snow and displayed all the pristine majesty of the God that created it, along with the mountains that surrounded it.

Alex placed his arm around Courtney's shoulder. His embrace was confirmation that the view they were experiencing together was magnificent. "This was a good idea, Alex. I believe you and I needed this distraction today, after the celestial event we witnessed last night," Courtney confessed.

"We know the moon is a sign, honey. It's a promise that our time here is coming to an end. The place he has prepared for us, well, I believe it will be more magnificent than this view."

The children gathered around their parents to bask in the warmth and love that was alive in each of them.

Chapter 48:
A Dream

THE BABY BUMP ON CINDY'S BELLY was starting to show. Tyler pulled up the tee shirt that once belonged to him, before she had taken possession of it, and placed the palm of his hand on her stomach. "It's a boy. I just know it's a boy this time," Tyler smiled with joy as he looked into Cindy's eyes.

"I had a dream last night. Our boy was at school, and he was being picked on by bullies. His sisters both came over to where their brother was, and saved him," Cindy laughed, as she told her story.

"Must be prophecy. There then, it's definitely a boy," Tyler responded to his wife.

Holding each other in an extended embrace, Tyler kissed Cindy. "I hope we get to see him. With the moon appearing as it did last night, I think the signs are clear," Cindy remarked with a somber look on her face.

Tyler smiled at her. "Even if we are taken home before the baby is born, he will be with us in heaven. We will see him, and be with him, for eternity," Tyler spoke these words to bring comfort to Cindy.

"I know, I know, but maybe, just maybe, we will be with our three girls for eternity," Cindy replied, as though she was a scholar speaking wisdom to a classroom.

Chapter 49:
The Trumpet

THE CAT PRODUCED AN EXTENDED STRETCH and bellowed a boisterous "meow" as loud as a cannon blast and the percussion that accompanied it. Gayland glanced down at his companion in acknowledgement of the animal's actions. The demon had felt uneasy all day. It was a feeling he had not experienced for quite some time, and he couldn't explain it away.

He stood up from his chair and pushed it enough to listen to the creaking sound it made. He was just about to retreat into the farmhouse to retrieve the frozen water that gave him so much pleasure when he noticed out in the distance, just outside the gate that gave entry to his sanctuary, was a figure he had not seen in a long time. Standing at the gate that read "NO TRESSPASSING" was the mortal persona of a large, bronze, Viking, sporting long braids of golden hair down his muscular back.

Then, with a thunderous tone that emitted from all around him, came an unmistakable sound. Gayland remembered it well from the time when he was an Angel in heaven. He remembered the golden horn that signaled the start of worship, except, this horn signaled something else.

It was the sound of a trumpet signaling the end.

Epilogue

WE ARE CURRENTLY LIVING IN THE CHURCH AGE, which marks the completion of these events: 1) the death of Christ; 2) the burial of Christ; 3) the resurrection of Christ; 4) the ascent of the Holy Spirit. The next event in God's calendar is the rapture when Jesus comes for His church.

"The Lord Himself will descend from heaven with a shout, with the voice of an archangel, and with the trumpet of God." 1 Thessalonians 4:16

The next event to unfold is the Tribulation, which occurs after all believers have been removed from earth at the rapture. The tribulation will last for seven years and will unveil totally unrestrained and unprecedented evil. Satan will be the great director of this deceit, utilizing evil in the flesh, in the form of the antichrist, aided by the false prophet. Despite Satan's attempt to execute his version of the Holy Trinity by immolating it, he will face his destiny, the second coming of Christ.

Jesus returns after the end of the Tribulation period, with His church to wage a final battle against all the enemies of God, who will be led by the beast and the false prophet, known as the battle of Armageddon. This battle and victory by our Lord and Savior will usher in the Millennium and believers will be given authority to reign with Him.

Satan is cast into the bottomless pit, shut up, so he shall deceive the nations no more for 1000 years.
Revelation 20: 1-7.

It has been my pleasure to tell the story of one such believer, a mortal man named Alex Dante, who will reign with Christ and his Angels in the Millennium as he is the keeper of the pit that binds Satan and his followers.
We all seek something. Some are seekers of truth, and some seek the lies that will benefit only them. Be a seeker of an eternity with God in glory.

www.ingramcontent.com/pod-product-compliance
Lightning Source LLC
Chambersburg PA
CBHW051803050726

47598CB00006B/2402